Praise for *Winter Damage*

'Elegantly lyrical … A heart-rending quest story about children in a bitterly cold, climate-changed Cornwall, searching for the everyday comforts and love of the world so recently lost'
Susan Elkin, *Independent*

'A tough, heart-breaking story of loss, fear and friendship'
We Love This Book

'A poetic, chilling and moving debut'
lovereading.com

'Small but perfectly formed, *Winter Damage* is the sort of book that begs to be read out loud, even if there's no one else near to hear it. It's a stone-cold stunner with an uncommonly humble heart, and I urge you to take it into yours, too'
Niall Alexander, *tor.com*

'A beautiful book. It's mysterious and lyrical, sad but hopeful, and truly unforgettable'
Top TeenReads 2013, *thebookbag.co.uk*

'Introducing a resourceful teenage heroine in bitter circumstances … This gripping quest tale is set in Cornwall in a near future suffering the effects of climate change and social collapse'
Geraldine Brennan, *Observer*

The LIGHT THAT GETS LOST

The LIGHT THat GETS LOST

NATASHA CARTHEW

BLOOMSBURY
LONDON OXFORD NEW YORK NEW DELHI SYDNEY

Bloomsbury Publishing, London, Oxford, New York, New Delhi and Sydney

First published in Great Britain in November 2015 by Bloomsbury Publishing Plc
50 Bedford Square, London WC1B 3DP

www.bloomsbury.com

Bloomsbury is a registered trademark of Bloomsbury Publishing Plc

A CIP catalogue record for this book is available from the British Library

ISBN 978 1 4088 3586 9

MIX
Paper from
responsible sources
FSC® C020471

Typeset by Integra Software Services Pvt. Ltd
Printed and bound in Great Britain by CPI Group (UK) Ltd, Croydon CR0 4YY

1 3 5 7 9 10 8 6 4 2

For Evelyn

CHAPTER ONE

Behind the slatted cupboard door the young boy adjusted his eyes to the dark and pressed his face to the tickle and cuddle of familiar coats. He could hear the shouting deep down in the belly of the house, a stranger's voice rolling thick with gravel stones, and he thought he heard his brother squeal and wished him quiet. Dad was churning up a storm, his low voice booming, steady, concentrating fear.

The boy knew it would be over soon. The man with the menace would be gone and the drum of kitchen pots and pans would mean Mum was getting the dinner on; the one good square meal with everyone sitting table tight. The boy smelt the trace of Mum's perfume in the oily fur of a coat she no longer wore and he petted the animal and pulled it to him.

In his imagination the first blast of gunfire was a TV cop show running too loud and Mum's shout a 'Too loud' warning to his brother. He couldn't help but smile. Big bro was taking a hit again, a whooper.

Stumbling footsteps climbed the wooden stairs and he plum-stuck his fingers into his ears when the shots grew louder. Noise ran into every door and the gun dumbed Mum first and then Dad and the boy imagined his brother dumbed down someplace other.

Everyone dumb and sitting silent, the TV shushed after all. He closed his eyes and pushed them into the guard his arms made and everything in him screamed for calm.

When calm came it was a long time in coming and the boy was slow to open his eyes. He peeked through the thin cracks between the wooden slats and in that moment perhaps he saw something of the man that was unforgettable and perhaps he heard something too.

He listened to the up-down of blood-stuck feet heel turn on the floorboards and head back downstairs and he pressed the animal version of Mum closer to his face until the tiny hairs filled his mouth and nose and he felt the flicker of a sneeze burn and water his eyes.

He begged the sneeze to stay away and swallowed it and pinched it gone and he listened out for the green flag of a slammed door and growing whispers, Mum and then Dad giving him the OK.

When was it safe to come out and why wasn't anyone saying it? A house fallen silent with three shots, four just about.

Through the cupboard door he could see dust fall like stars in the room of recent commotion, the sun just snagging, revealing. Mum was flat out on the floor. She'd spilt something and was caught in a half-thought going under the bed.

'Mum,' the boy whispered. 'Mum, get up.' He moved his hand from the slats and put a foot to the door. Standing in the sticky he shouted over and when she didn't move he kicked her leg hard, once then twice. The sticky was growing and it branched out like creeping fingers into the fancy rug and the boy shouted for her not to go but it was too late, the bed had her.

Out in the hall there was nothing but big boot memories and the boy jumped the stairs and if he fell into the gunman's arms then it would be fate that put him there. Where was the man with the one last bullet? The bullet with the boy's name scratched on it. Mum was gone and Dad was somewhere gone and his brother Billy was a meat lump with more crawling sticky in the front room, glanced at as he ran from the house.

He ran flat out hard and fast. Ran until his legs shook heavy with burn and his feet no longer felt the rub and blister of bare tramping. He ran a blind course through the first cut of hay in the fields that were always going brown, then green, then gold. He took himself clean through hedges and half of skin and summer clothes were left behind.

The boy found himself at the edge of the cliffs just as the sun settled out beyond the headland and he watched the fire free-fall into the sea as if for the first and last time, a thing of beauty come too late, a butterfly caught in hand and held too tight, its colour rubbed to dust. He stood until the orange and the red receded and sat with the blue and flash of night sky stars and when the dark of real night came he lay in the black and listened to the crash and draw of a rising tide.

Something in the dark claimed the boy that night. A needling hook of skulking roots that pulled him towards some other place; an underhanded, underground grasp. A little demon settling someplace deep inside, a flicker-flame moving, growing in size.

Eight years later

Trey sat at the back of the van and watched the outside world lope past through wire mesh windows. An indifferent landscape that moved independently from his erratic thinking, it was both beautiful and dangerous. A thin film of wet ocean fog stampeded towards the moor and he watched it grease the pane of glass until there was nothing left for looking. He called out to the social worker sat slouched up front and asked what time they would arrive but the man ignored him and instead bent to tune the radio to local news. Trey pulled up the hood on his jacket and when the van filled with the screams of scally town kids running riot he covered his ears completely. He leant his head against the window with one eye spying the rain and what water leaked there he let soak and pool in his hair and felt it run down his cheek and enjoyed the momentary cool. His short life, sketched and drawn wrong since memory began, had been rubbed down to this one moment in time; he was sitting at the brink of a place where there was no turning back and he was ready to jump. For Mum and Dad and Billy he was ready to leap into the unknown and all he knew of that unknown was it had one single solitary name and the name was revenge.

He saw his mum in his imaginings and he told her he would do the thing that needed doing and perhaps he said it out loud, and if he did he didn't care because this was it, he was going in.

'Camp Kernow,' shouted the man suddenly. 'Welcome to your new home.'

Trey kicked forward to look out of the window and he rubbed the condensation from the glass with the heel of his hand and through the hammering rain he saw the fence fill the darkening morning with bright-light diamonds.

'You'll learn a trade here boy, farmin or butcherin or such. Your last foster home was a farm, you like animals, don't you?'

Trey ignored him.

'You're lucky to be comin here. Might not think it yet but them runnin this place got religion on their side, them sellin salvation. You listenin, Trey boy? Got God championin you here.'

The boy nodded. He knew this already and it made him smile knowing it. This was the place where things were about to rewind to the point of wrong and settle back right.

He watched the social worker wind down his window as they approached the gate and the boy turned to study the ten-foot razor-wire fence that loomed overhead and the armed guard that took his time to climb down from his tower. The guard stood at the window and took up the ID papers and then bent to look at the boy in the back seat.

Trey knew he looked like all boys cut from the same rag and when the man nodded towards him he looked down. If there was something in Trey's eyes that might give himself away, he did not know. But the van lurched forward and he was glad of it in any case.

The van parked in a skid at the front of a clapboard farmhouse and Trey pushed down into the seat and he picked his fingers and bit at them for the chew. He watched the social worker stand to attention on the porch. The 'Welcome' sign that was tied there swung out when he knocked. Trey tried to make something of the place that was to be his home for the summer and he set his mind ready for clues. Out there in the muddied wet was the murderer, a man who thought he was safe in the cloth of God, but he was not.

Trey looked down at his hands and sighed. He'd drawn blood from the pull of flesh from his thumb and he pushed the wet into his jeans to soak it dry. He watched the windows of the house for movement and he watched the door like a hawk and when it opened he bubbled his breath deep down into his chest. So close now, he could smell the caustic anger burn and fizz inside and he blanked his face for the show of indifference.

He waited for the door lock to disengage and took his time to step from the van and he went towards the men on the porch with the rain heavy on his shoulders and his rucksack held baby tight in his arms.

He stood out of the rain and waited for the social worker to introduce him to a man known simply as McKenzie. Trey nodded and smiled and hoped that he gave nothing of himself away except the usual bad boy, sorry boy, any boy.

When McKenzie reached out a hand Trey shook it and he wished he'd thought to wipe the sweat-slip from it first.

'This guy here is head of all things managerial. You listen to him and follow his lead and you won't go wrong.'

Trey looked at the man and he searched his face for a telltale clue. 'You a Preacher?' he asked and he coughed to get the shake from his throat.

The man shook his head and said he was a superintendent of sorts and he told him to stand before him.

'Don't worry I int gonna bite.' McKenzie laughed and he told Trey to stretch his arms and legs.

'Just lookin for knives and drugs and whatever else. Turn out your pockets.'

Trey did what he was told and he was glad that he'd thought to hide his lighter in his trainer.

'You smoke?' McKenzie asked.

'Yes, sir.'

'Well not any more, you don't.'

He invited them to sit on the porch and the two men chose seats either side of Trey, fake guardians and protectors and more. They discussed the best way for Trey to knuckle down to institutional life and he nodded and tried not to slouch in the low wooden chair. Truth was he'd known nothing but his entire life and he thought about the run of promises arranged in his open palms like a string of dodgy pearls.

He would do everything asked of him, he promised the men this, and he promised himself and most of all he promised the demon that was forever watchful inside.

'I bin told you're a hard worker.' The man nodded and a whip of thin white hair fell into his face and stuck to his beard.

'Yes, sir.'

'Good strong worker by all accounts. Could do with that roundabouts.'

Trey shrugged and he wanted to say something kind of truthful but the two men were talking to each other in any case. They slung comments into the air like warning shots for bravado's sake and Trey wondered if this was something about being a man that he should learn. Smiling and saying the right things in the wrong order, clubbed forward with hands gripped and flicking. He wondered if he might trust the skinny, watchful man, trust him proper and not just for the sake of dependence. He watched his eyes dart about like twinned river fish and when he caught Trey's eye he winked.

'So you like animals?' He smiled. 'Hope you like cattle cus cattle is all we got, just about.'

He looked at Trey with curiosity circling and nodded and told him to head to the bunkhouses to find his house master.

Trey pulled the family photo from out his rucksack when McKenzie told him to leave it on the porch step and he tucked it into the back pocket of his jeans. He stood and scuffed his boots on the wooden deck for thinking time. He wanted to ask about the bunkhouse's whereabouts but the two men were already head down to paperwork and bank notes.

Trey stepped off the porch and into puddles and noticed for the first time that it had stopped raining.

He circled the ramshackle farmhouse and cut across the clearing beside it and he didn't bother with direction because he didn't know where he was going or who he was supposed to find in any case.

'We're in,' he said to himself. He hoped Mum and Dad in heaven heard and Billy in the nursing home and he knew the demon inside heard because he whispered, 'Good job.'

Trey could almost lick revenge from off his lips, could taste the bittersweet and it tasted good.

He looked around him at the tracks in the wet clay dirt and at the inroads that rose with thick tyre treads used to pulling heavy loads. Trey tailed the skids and he wondered about the corrugated iron barns that were everywhere and he listened out for the sound of other kids but heard nothing but the distant turn of generators and the cry of cows that horned from every direction.

He kicked at the track that passed the farmhouse and followed its vertical scar up a ridge to its highest point and when he reached the top he bent in half until the air returned to his lungs.

The camp below stretched out before him and was vast, a scatter of junk and rock and unyielding earth and everything tumbling towards the only thing to stop it dead – the fence.

Behind him a tree stump had been hacked into a rough set seat and Trey sat and looked down on to the sandy plain and the pockmarks scarred with trenches and cordons and boundaries. The social worker had told him that for the next six months this would be home and work and life and Trey couldn't wait to cut and edge beneath its skin and settle within.

He shuffled his feet amongst the butt ends that encircled the stump and traced a finger into the smooth dip of a hundred initials burnt into its flesh and he wished he'd asked to stop at some store for cigarettes to hide in his other shoe before being planted in the middle of moor. He reached for a butt and kicked off his trainer and took out his lighter and he lit the butt and smoked what was left, along with the damp earth clinging to it, until his throat became too tight for bothering.

He looked down at the camp with the clay-cut yard and the four tin-shack houses arranged on either side and the marquee tent behind and his eyes traced the fence as far as he could see, searching for the corners and finding none.

He could see a scatter of farm buildings at the left of the camp and beyond that rough fields squared into the rock earth. In the distance he saw cows and calves idling, oblivious to the steal-drum building close to Trey that smoked black and stank of bad burn.

Trey sighed and he flicked his lighter at the tree stump to scorch a rub of black into it and he wondered about burning things like he did most days. It was good to think things over, put some kind of finish to his thinking. Trey was forever waiting to get back to the start line, the start of his life as it was meant to be.

He painted a picture of himself and Billy settled down by the sea, an old scrap-built hut for bedding down and a boat pitching in the bay. They'd fish for anything worth bartering. Billy was a genius with a hook and line, and they'd sit out front on the trampled sand and watch the sun set and come good again, a night spent eating mackerel and drinking whatever. Two boys closer in age now than their seven years, two boys idling under a crescent moon, forever brothers, forever free.

Trey couldn't wait to get the revenge thing pared from his bones; he would set the demon free and go spring Billy from the care home all in one swoop. He wondered what it would be like to live out his days without the fire balling in his belly, have the cool calm wash over him, soothe him; he couldn't imagine it for all the revenge that coursed through his veins.

He ran his fingers over the metal lighter that was not meant to be in his possession. He wasn't to go looking for fire – that was part of the deal, the social worker said – but Trey was all for small steps, rehabilitation in tiny doses, drip therapy.

He considered trying for another cigarette and thought better of it and he surveyed the land beneath him for signs of life and there were none and instead he made his way back down the hill towards the buildings.

He couldn't remember who he was supposed to look for and he stood and shouted out for anybody but only his lesser self called back.

He looked at his watch and sighed. It was a little past eleven in the morning and he supposed everyone was at work. He kicked at the ground and at the marks his trainers made in the wet sucking earth and continued back towards the farmhouse. He stepped up to the porch to look for the men but they had long gone and he searched for his bag but that had gone too.

He stood a moment and looked towards the gates and the two guards planted on platforms either side, their guns facing outward towards some unknown threat.

'You lost, boy?' came a voice from inside the house and Trey jumped from the porch.

He jammed his hands into his pockets and watched as eyes appeared through the dark web screen door and he was close to running when the voice told him to stay put.

'Spose you think this is some sort of holiday camp, strollin round and whatever.'

'I'm lookin for someone.' He coughed.

'Who?'

'Can't right remember, a house master.'

'Well that int no good.'

Trey pushed his hands deeper into his pockets and his left hand tightened to smooth comfort.

'Master what?'

'Dunno, sir. That McKenzie said go lookin.'

A stout, muscular man came to the door and he folded his arms and he looked like he was settling to stand there a good while.

'Go lookin, up and down and roundabout, that kind of lookin?'

Trey shrugged and he took his time to trace the outline of the man for possible clues, make an imprint that he could go over later.

'Well int that funny?' The man stepped closer. 'Cus you're halfway doin right without even tryin. New boy, int you?' He reached out a hand and Trey shook it and the man mangled and mashed the wet from it and he introduced himself as his house master.

He stood back and looked Trey up and over the same way he might regard cattle on market day. 'You can call me DB or sir and I spose I can call you what I want.'

Trey wanted to ask after the social worker to make a connection of things known and he thought about his bag with the little knick-knack things that would mean nothing to a man like this and he asked what had happened to it.

'Locked up no doubt, locked up same as the rest of the crap.' He left the confines of the doorframe and stepped off the porch in a stretch. 'But I'd say that int where your worry is right now.'

Trey thought about the nothing things he could do without and the family things he couldn't and he was glad of the photo folded neatly in his back pocket.

'You know where my bag is?' he asked again and the demon told him to stay put until he got what was his but the man had turned his back and he shouted for him to follow as he walked towards the yard with the bunkhouses all around.

'This is Tavy house, one of four bunkhouses as it stands. Tavy, Tamar, Lynner and Plym. The kids call them what they want no doubt but Tavy is this one's name and the name stays.'

Trey stood at the open door and peered through the wall of heat that punched tipsy from the room and he waited for his eyes to adjust to the change in light.

'What you think?' The man laughed.

'It's hot.'

'Course it's hot. Rain's stopped and sun's out, init? Hottest summer since forever and it int even begun and here we got a metal roof and the walls is metal so what you reckon, it's hot.'

Trey stepped into the room and he looked over the rows of beds so close together there was barely room for squeezing.

'Any questions?' the man asked.

Trey shrugged.

'You gotta have questions.'

Trey racked his brain but every question seemed out of bounds and instead he asked where he should put his things.

'What things?'

'Clothes and stuff?'

'Clothes go on the shelves above. Stuff stays locked up until such time as you earn it.'

'What do I do to earn it, sir?'

'Search me. Preacher's the one who makes the rules, I just keep you in line.' He looked at Trey and his eyes settled on his wrist. 'And you can hand that over while we're at it.'

Trey looked down at his wrist and he told the man the watch was his dad's. He wanted to explain that it was a present from Mum on their wedding day and had their initials and the date inscribed on the back and everything. He looked up at the man. More than anything he wanted to tell him Dad was dead. Maybe if he told him he would let him keep it.

'Well?' he said. 'Hand it over.'

Trey rubbed his thumb over the glass face of the watch, but he knew he couldn't risk telling about Dad and Mum and so he bent the clip and undid the clasp and handed it to the man.

'Don't worry, you'll get it back, spose you will anyway.' The man laughed and when he jammed the watch into his pocket the demon inside of Trey warmed from this fuel and fuel was good; they needed it for their fire.

Trey stood small-boy fierce in the room of hot air and when they heard the sound of voices approaching the building the man told him to choose a place to sleep.

'And hurry up. Int unusual for newbies to sleep on the floor.'

Trey looked around him and sat on the nearest bed to try the bounce and it was nothing much except a thin roll of padding and board beneath.

He thought about the best bed to choose given his situation and he walked the small corrugated room and every corner was as hot as the next.

He heard the skid of wheels in the dust outside and caught the fine scent of diesel and he picked the bed nearest the door despite the scatter of clothes on the floor and he wrote his name at the top of the form that clung to a clipboard at its foot.

Outside he was glad to replace the claustrophobic heat with the heat of day. The sun was coming good and making flint-splits in the clouds and he joined the whip trail of dust and exhaust fumes that headed downhill away from the bunkhouses.

A group of boys walked up ahead and there was something about their lived-in swagger that told Trey to hang back.

He wasn't like these other boys. His life had been set upon by circumstances beyond his control. He wasn't bad for the kick of things; he'd grown bad like bacteria on foul meat.

He took his time to circle his way to wherever it was they were meant and he kept his head down to keep from looking at anyone the wrong way.

Midday was approaching and with it came a pinch of pain at the back of his neck that could only be the slow nip of sunburn and Trey rubbed it with his hand and wished he had the smarts to have hooked his cap from out his bag earlier.

He kept his eyes on his clumsy feet and tried to ignore the footsteps that almost clipped his heels from behind.

'You're gettin burnt,' said a small voice and Trey ignored it.

'Bubblin right up it is, like pizza.'

Trey sped up despite the lads up ahead and all their footsteps fell in line like marching men.

'What we got 'ere?' laughed one of the boys. 'Where the other five dwarfs?'

Everyone laughed and Trey turned to look at the tall, fat boy beside him.

'You come as a pair?' The boy continued and he lifted his fringe to get a good look at Trey. 'Only it looks like you do. A pair of circus freaks, I'd say.'

Trey shrugged at the nothing joke. There were worse things to be called than small. He looked at the other boy who, unlike Trey, was thin and brittle and he moved off to keep association at bay.

'I'm Larry,' said the reedy boy and he followed Trey towards the clearing that surrounded the tent.

Trey nodded and when he saw others sit down on the scatter of rough-sawn benches he did the same and he hoped the thin boy would go away. A boy like that was sore-thumb trouble, he knew that as fact. Trey wanted more than anything to ignore the yappy boy. He knew all about incarceration from his stint in young offenders, knew that you should avoid the needy like the plague; their weakness could rub off and on to you.

He glanced at the boy and something inside felt sorry for him. He hated that.

'I said my name's Larry.' The boy waited for Trey to reply and when he didn't he elbowed him in the ribs.

'What?' asked Trey.

'I'm talkin to you.'

'And?'

'Least you can do is talk back.'

'Leave me alone.'

'High and mighty, int you? Thought you could do with a friend out here in the middle, make it easier bein the newbie and all.'

Trey ignored the boy. He wasn't bothered about getting along with anyone for the sake of company. He had all he needed in memory and fantasy combined.

'You're new,' the boy continued. 'I know you're new cus I know all the goss in this place, just bout anyway.'

The boy leant forward to look at Trey and he was a long time looking. 'You gonna tell me your name then?' he asked.

Trey shrugged. 'Tremain,' he said. 'Tremain Pearce. Most call me Trey.'

'I'm Larry but I told you that, in any case all call me Lamby.'

Trey glanced at the boy and he had 'odd' sugar-rock written right through him. 'What name you like best?' he asked.

'Does it matter?'

Trey shrugged and sat back to watch the boys and a fistful of girls settle to the circle of benches and he asked the boy what was happening.

'Intros, rules and regs,' the boy continued. 'Usual show for you newbies, which today is just you. It's all bull.'

'How many new kids you get a month?'

'Depends.'

'On what?'

'How many got out last month.'

'How many was that?'

'One, only one. That's why it's just you. Anyway, all you got to remember is don't and double don't.'

'Don't what?'

'Speak, think, ask questions, that sort of thing.'

Trey sat expectantly, examining the men that stepped up on to the stacking-pallet stage in front of the tent but nothing about them reminded him of his parents' killer.

'What church them all from anyway?'

'Dunno proper. Don't think them all's from a church in the conventional sense. None of that nicey, like you'd think, them stricter, I spose. The Preacher is the head, set it up backalong.'

'So it's his church?' asked Trey. 'He made it up?'

'Spose.'

Trey watched the three men on the stage fiddle with a megaphone and he kept his eyes stuck to them despite the stinging sour smoke that meandered through the camp.

He had a million questions to ask but when he went to speak the boy held up his hand and looked back at the stage.

A man that called himself camp chaplain had taken to the stage and Trey watched the old man attempt to quieten the crowd and he tried to concentrate on his voice. Frail or no, Trey could not risk letting anyone fall beneath his radar.

He closed his eyes and turned his ear to every note and sound, but as always his mind took to wandering and he realised his finger-picking had again drawn blood. He pressed the small wound against his thigh and when the bleeding didn't stop he asked Lamby if he had a tissue and when the boy ignored him he asked again. Trey was slow to realise that the chaplain had been replaced by McKenzie and the crowd had fallen silent with everyone sat turned in their seats, forty plus pairs of eyes looped and settling on Trey. McKenzie coughed for attention and he asked him to tell the others his name. He told him to stand on the bench and shout it. Trey stood and stepped up and he shouted loud and his voice cracked with embarrassment.

'Tremain,' said the man.

Trey nodded and he dangled with the demon coiled inside.

'Don't look so scared. Int you bin told we're one happy family?'

Trey was not sure if it was a question he had been asked and he looked down at his feet with the fall-apart trainers and they wanted to run.

'Well?' asked the man.

Trey shrugged. His head spun with the right/wrong words to say and the demon shouted something that made it hard to hear. He looked up at the man and shrugged again and the other kids gasped at his insolence.

'I'll see you later, Rudeboy,' said McKenzie. 'Sit down.'

Trey sat with the red of stupid burning in his cheeks and his neck almost in flames. He watched the sea of heads snap to attention and he wished for a hole to open up and suck him in. He flicked the blood from his dripping finger on to the stubborn earth and he looked the crowd over to see if anyone was bold enough to still be turned his way and there was.

A girl who looked about his age sat half bent towards the stage and she looked at him with curiosity and it was as if there was something between them that was a known thing. Trey looked away and was quick to glance at his hands for the refuge and he listened to the man who thought himself boss big himself up and he sat as stiff as the boy at his side.

Trey had been pinned hard to the ground and he knew it, pinned and tied and labelled with a stupid name and all because of something and nothing much. He didn't fall in with things the way other kids did. He had too much chat in his head; some days he couldn't hear much more than what went on in his mind. He wished he could set fire to his thinking, blow the ash into the cluttered corners like a spring clean and start over.

He rubbed his eyes and set them to the stage where the chaplain had taken to the deck for prayers and Trey listened to the good-god words and said them over when asked because he really did want to fit in.

His eyes sought out DB and Dad's watch stuffed any-old in his pocket and he reminded himself that he would be a good boy, a better boy than any of the other boys. If he was to have any chance of finding out the truth he had to keep to the rules and gain the masters' trust no matter that he hated them all; trust meant an open road to revenge.

When their names were roll-called into houses they were told they had ten minutes of loose time before lining up and Trey stood because he thought better that way.

'Isn't this great?' grinned Lamby. 'We're in the same house. Imagine that. Begsy the bed next to you.'

Trey shook his head and said 'Whatever' and he looked over to where the girl had been sitting.

'Spose you think this place is strict,' said Lamby.

'Not really.'

'Don't lie, anyway they can't afford to have it any other way. Lost boys, we are. Int that what they call us, society I mean?'

Trey didn't care what 'they' called them; he'd given up on society in the same way that it had given up on him and those like him a long time ago, but he guessed the boy was right.

A ragtag line of damaged kids running crazy across the nation's terrain just about described them, a layer of loose sediment free falling.

'Spose I don't care long as I learn a trade, do my time.' He looked at the boy and shrugged. Lying came easy to him.

'Really? You serious?' Lamby laughed but stopped when he saw Trey's expression. 'Is that what you bin told? Learn a trade and get a qually and a job?'

'Maybe.' Trey turned his back. There was something slippery strange about the boy and he wondered why he insisted on shortening every other word down to nothing.

'Good luck in any case,' the boy shouted after him. 'Maybe you'll be a lucky un, who knows?'

Trey hoped he'd still be allowed to do farming like he'd been told and a little good nature came to him and it went just as fast when he saw McKenzie beckon to him from across the clearing.

'Rudeboy,' he shouted.

Trey kept quiet. He knew it was best.

'Rudeboy, answer me.'

'Yes, sir.' Trey nodded some kind of truce.

McKenzie looked him up and looked him down and he rubbed what hair he had with a whip of excitement.

'You got a problem with authority, boy? Cus your social worker dint say nothin bout that.'

'No, sir.'

'No, sir, what?'

'No, sir, I int got a problem with authority, sir.'

McKenzie put his hands in his pockets and jangled his chain and keys in a mix.

'Gonna like workin with you, boy. I reckon I'm gonna enjoy ropin you in. What work you say you fancy?'

'Farm, sir, lookin after livestock.'

'Like that, would you?'

'Yes, sir.'

McKenzie started to laugh. 'I'd use the term "farm" loosely if I were you. Trenches and fences with cattle thrown in is nearer the mark. Sure you don't wanna do slaughter? Could do with a stocky lad like you down the slaughterhouse.'

Trey smiled; there was no shame about it.

'Good boy, Rudeboy.'

Up close the man smelt of cigars and cheap-seat after-shave and Trey searched his childhood memory for anything of him. They were all holy men after all. They all belonged to the same fanatical church.

'Well run along, there's a good boy.'

Trey returned to the crowd and he allowed himself a little flicker flame anger to rise up within and he wished for one brief moment that he had something to burn and blow outright for the hell of it.

'Slaughter's as bad as it sounds if you was wonderin. You wanna stay away from slaughter.'

Trey stopped and scanned the surrounding faces until he saw the girl and his head spun with the panic and complication brought on by sudden beauty.

'I wanted to do farm,' he blurted. 'Who'd I have to see?'

'I was told to introduce myself by the chaplain, so here I am introducin myself. I'm Kay, I do farm.'

Trey nodded and she told him that the chaplain was the only master worth anything and to remember that.

'I int thought much of the others, that's for sure.' He smiled and asked her what house she was in.

'Lynner, all ten girls is Lynner. Boys is Tamar, Tavy or Plym, them named after rivers.' She shrugged for the 'whatever' and Trey shrugged too.

'Don't worry, McKenzie was just windin you up. If you was assigned farm then that's where you'll be, for now anyway.'

They walked the crowd and found Lamby without looking and soon the idling time was up and they were told to get into their house groups.

'Rudeboy,' laughed DB outside Tavy. 'I like it and I dint even make it up.'

Trey nodded. 'I'm called Trey,' he said and he tried to smile and he bit down on the stupid name and the stupid rules.

'Int gonna cry over it like some mother's boy, is you?'

Trey swallowed hard to keep the demon in. 'No, sir, I int no mother's boy, sir,' he lied.

'Well int that good to hear. Now go get your clothes.'

Trey nodded.

Outside the tin hut dorm he waited to receive the shabby camp-issue garments. Two T-shirts, two vests and a shirt, all grey, plus cap, grey.

'Is this it?' he asked the boy who stood guard over the open suitcase.

'Why, what else you want? You can wear what you like on your legs, big swishy skirt if you want.'

'You're funny.' Trey rubbed his fingers over the cheap material and what was left of nail caught in the fabric.

'So are you,' sneered the boy. 'Now do one.'

Trey went into the bunkhouse and threw the clothes on to the bed he'd picked and he lay among them and wondered if he might ask for work boots because the second-hand trainers that stuck to his feet had seen better days. He linked his hands behind his head and he wished Mum was around to give him some indication of right from wrong so he could set his mind to what he needed to know.

'Why you loungin bout?' asked Lamby. 'This int free time.'

'I thought it was long as we stayed in our house groups?'

'Outside,' giggled Lamby. 'Free time long as we stay in our house groups outside. The masters like to keep an eye on us.'

'I wanted to rest.'

'Well you can't cus we gotta go barbecue. It's one o'clock, dumb-poke.' Lamby reached out a hand to pull him to his feet and Trey ignored it.

'Camp's just bout the best fun a kid can have,' Lamby continued. 'One big happy family apparently.'

Trey stayed put and he kept his fingers locked behind his head a moment longer. He closed his eyes and for one shutter second he pictured the four of them on the beach.

Mum, Dad, Billy and himself the day before the shooting, a happy family nothing family. For eight years he had waited for this moment to arrive. He was doing this for them.

CHAPTER TWO

Outside in the clearing Trey joined the other kids and each one took the miserly offering of thin-skin meat and bread sandwich. He sat cross-legged in the drying dust dirt and tried to keep his distance from the irritating Lamby and he listened in on the other boys' conversations and smiled at their jokes and he wished he had a pack of cigarettes to share to ease his new-boy pain.

The boys in Tavy house were all same-as in background to Trey. Poor white trash with stories all in a jumble the same. Some had criminal records and some were just plain criminal. Each one sat bolted with fear and front, trying hard not to reveal the vulnerability inside. Trey noticed this in each boy and he noticed it in himself, every boy that was apart from one, the teasing boy from earlier, the boy they called Wilder.

Wilder had a mouth like winter, spiteful and spitting and taut with opinion. He had something to say about everything and Trey thought he might just bust with the pressure of words in his head and on his tongue and all in all he was bullish and Trey didn't like him and neither did his demon.

'So what you got to say for yourself, Rudeboy?' The boy spat out his words through gums thick with meat. 'Say somethin funny, somethin rude.'

Trey took his time to chew on the tasteless twang burger and he kept his eyes peeled all ways to assess his surroundings. No matter what he thought about Wilder, it was obvious he was held in some kind of high regarding light by the others and it wasn't his stature or opinion that held them captivated, but something else. Something Trey couldn't work out but needed to understand in order to get the better of the boy.

'You not talkin to your little friend here no more? Cus I think you two make a great double act. Should be in the circus, couple of squirts like you.'

The other boys rustled up a half-hearted laugh between them and Trey laughed too because a truce was an easier route to settling in. He told himself he wasn't here for trouble with the other kids and he told the demon in case he'd forgotten to remember the same.

'You're hilarious,' he said at last and his voice sounded funny, not used to conversation.

Wilder nodded and he leant back on his hands and stretched his feet out towards Trey's face. 'So he does talk. How bout that, boys. The Rudeboy has a voice.'

'Tremain.' He cleared his throat. 'My name's Tremain.'

Wilder shook his hand like the man he thought he should be, tough and powerful and the leader of things.

'You just as well get used to your new name cus it int likely we'll remember the other one.

Old McKenzie still has it in him for a top nickname, no matter how much of an ass he might be.'

Trey shrugged. 'You got one?' he asked.

'What?'

'A nickname.'

Wilder shook his head. 'He wouldn't dare, knows who I am well enough, knows how things work on the outside.'

They passed around a non-brand bottle of cola and some boys sucked and sighed with the pretence that it was something stronger.

'My dad's rich as hell,' Wilder continued. 'Owns all sorts of businesses.'

The boy looked at Trey and smiled and a tiny shard of something other quick-flashed in his eyes and Trey wondered if this father thing was something he might keep tooled away for later, a bit of ammo that might come in handy.

'Anyway, this is Anders,' continued Wilder. 'Anders, pass him the bottle.'

Trey took up the bottle and passed it over to Lamby to avoid the beef and bread backwash and he asked Wilder what work he did in camp.

31

'Anythin I want.'

'Whatever takes his fancy,' added Anders.

'But right now, well, I think I'll go back to slaughterin for the fun. I've done butcherin, borin, logistics, borin so it was back to slaughter or stinky farm work.'

'I'm on slaughterin too,' said Anders. 'Worst is farmin.'

Trey looked down Anders' fat legs splayed flat against the earth and the tumble of belly in his lap and he asked what he'd worked at before slaughter.

'Kitchen.' The boy grinned. 'And I was really good at it, but someone had me moved.'

'He ate all the food,' laughed Wilder.

Trey wondered what else he might ask to keep the boys from questioning him and he thought about the job of butcher and asked if it was the same as slaughter work.

'Course it is,' answered Anders.

'No it int,' said Wilder. 'Not rightly anyway. Slaughterin is your basic killin and butcherin is the chop-shop. There int much fun in chop-shop.'

Trey nodded and he thought about the fun that was gleaned from killing and his heart hurt thinking it.

When the bell rang to indicate silent prayer Trey was glad of the calm and he closed his eyes to keep from looking at the boot heel digging into his side.

'Here we go,' said Wilder. 'Chaplain's on his high horse again; love thy neighbour and all that, weirdo.'

They sat in a puddle of contemplation and sweat and when the chaplain told them they were allowed to mingle Trey said he needed to stretch his legs so he could be on his own. There was one thing worse than being with people and that was being with people you didn't know. He liked to get the measure of them, sus them, work out what they wanted to hear and have them hear it to keep from opening up about himself.

He walked a little way out from the clearing and found the path he'd taken earlier, changing route near the ridge precipice towards a scratch of nothing land which brought him through a circle of stunted trees that stabbed the dead clay earth like a violent afterthought.

He touched the crippled trunks as he walked and his mind kicked over the day's events with his thoughts stumbling over the faces of the men he had seen. He wished he'd got the chance to catch sight of all the masters. Beyond the trees he stopped to view the land below and he thought about the bully boys and for the first time he realised what the summer would really be like.

He scrutinised the huge gorged tracks that cut into the difficult land and they snaked and tailed all ways and stretched as far as the eye could see. Out on the north horizon where earlier the mist had shrouded he could see metal barns the size of airport hangars melt and jiggle in the heat. He looked for shade and found a line of shadow spearing from one of the bigger trees and sat on the damp earth.

Trey knew there would be no time for idling; this was a get-in get-out type of place. Sniff out his parents' killer and do the one-trick job the demon had planned for him.

'You int meant to leave the clearin.'

Trey jumped suddenly when he saw Kay appear through the trees and he tucked the bad thoughts that rattled him neatly back inside.

'I int meant to leave either, difference is I don't care and you should.' She lit a cigarette and sat down beside him. 'Mad, init? The constant prayin and all them rules, even these stupid same-as uniforms.'

Trey smiled because her T-shirt had the sleeves cut from it and had faded to the colour of silver sand.

'Yours int too bad,' he noted.

'You get used to washin em most days, soon fade out.'

Trey nodded. 'I spose.'

They sat and watched the drift of occasional cloud bump merry as they scooped the horizon and their shadows were like ghost cars rallying mindless across the divide.

'Spose you think it's not so bad here,' she said and she kept her eyes on the horizon. 'Give it a few days and you won't think much more'n escapin.'

Trey rubbed his trainers into the stubborn ground and said at least the view was better than four concrete walls.

'We got plenty of em too, corrugated iron ones if you int noticed.'

'Buildins and bunkers is everywhere. I've seen the bunkhouses but what's in em others?'

'That building next to the dorms is the activity hut and em bigger ones behind is the slaughterhouse and furnace and butchery, and the farmhouse at the entrance to camp is where the masters and the chaplain live. Everything else is storage just cus.' She looked at Trey to check that he was keeping up.

'You see that tiny barn on the horizon?' she asked.

Trey squinted to see where she was pointing.

'That's the farm stables.' She took a long pull of her cigarette and passed it to him. As she continued to look out on the vista Trey took a moment to memorise her profile. It was akin to watching the serenity of an incoming tide settle to rock and stone.

'So what you in for?' She turned to catch him watching and disappointment was a brief whip-slap flash across her face.

Trey shook his head and his hand went to the heat pain at the back of his neck. 'Seems like forever ago, more even.'

'Was it?'

'Spose not.' He took a long pull of the cigarette.

'So what then?'

He didn't like to go over the list of whats and whens that had got him into camp. It had been a needs-must thing that had to be done. It should have been a secret and with anyone else it might have, but there was something about Kay that was set right and he knew from this one day of meeting that he could trust her.

'It was a stupid thing,' he said. 'A mistake type thing, I spose.'

'Go on.'

'It was a crazy thing. I wish it never happened,' he lied.

'We all wish that.'

Trey sighed, he didn't reckon on this. 'My foster home,' he blurted. 'Burnt it down to dust in the ground. That's bout the whole of it.'

Kay shrugged.

'It's a long story if you was wonderin.'

'I int. It's your story, yours to keep.'

Trey wanted to tell her everything because she didn't want to know anything. He wanted to tell the puzzling girl about his parents and his brother and all the events that led to this new chapter in his life, shuffling and stumbling out on a precipice. The truth was he didn't know what he was doing in all the ways of knowing something.

He had thought things through enough to commit to a deed so bad he'd get banged up somewhere way worse than any young offenders; the place where he would get revenge, he'd got that far in his thinking.

'The balance is whether you killed anyone or no.'

'No. Well, did kill two horses but that was cus part of the stables caught fire. I dint mean to do that bit.'

'That's bad,' she said and she clicked her boot heels one two on the ground.

'I know.'

'I bloody love horses.'

'Sorry.' He passed back the cigarette.

They sat in silence and Trey thought up stuff to say that was more than bubble words and he asked her if they ever got to do other things.

'What you mean?'

'Do stuff besides workin.'

Kay shook her head. 'Course not, but farmin int so bad.' She started to talk about the horses that were kept in the stables over at the farm block and Trey leant against the tree to listen.

He didn't know much about girls because of his shyness, but there was something about this girl that was different. She was everything other girls weren't, tough-stitched and confident, and she acted like she didn't have the time for much. Trey liked that. He didn't have time for much either.

'I get to spend most evenins with em.' She shrugged. 'It's extra work but it beats all else.'

Trey watched the last of the cloud shadows disperse and the sun head someplace other than the north sky they were looking at. He imagined Kay riding fast across the plain and her long black hair trailing like tyre smoke and he smiled because that image suited her and sat right with him.

'So you want to do farm work?' she asked.

'Hope it don't get changed cus I was talkin. Don't like the thought of slaughterin and butcherin and whatever else.'

'McKenzie would have swapped you by now if he was gonna do it,' said Kay. 'Don't beat yourself up. Most things in this dump is bout logistics, packin, storin and movin and not much else.'

'What's logistics?'

'Loadin meat into trucks and drivin A to B, you never get to leave the compound, just up to the boundary fence and back. I got to do it for a while when the camp first opened before they started to make all the rules.'

'How long you bin here?'

'Long enough.'

'How long?'

When Kay ignored him Trey asked what got moved around.

'Animals, dead ones, I said that already.'

'I knew I'd be workin but dint think that was all.'

'Why? Dint they say you'd learn a trade or somethin?'

Trey nodded. 'Spose.'

'And who's gonna argue the toss if we're learnin or workin or whatever? Long as we're locked up, society can pretend we don't exist, int that how it goes?'

Trey shrugged and said the regime had got worse on the outside. 'Don't get no warnins or nothin now if you do one thing wrong, not since the unrest last winter and all that. You gotta be off the streets by six and if you int you get slammed by the army.' He wanted to say how it had worked in his favour, but to any normal person this would have sounded crazy. Nobody wanted to be locked up except for him.

'Least we get a day off tomorrow,' he said.

Kay got up and brushed the damp dust from her legs. 'What you mean?'

'Sunday, init?'

'Dint I just say we don't get no time off?'

Trey got up and he hated the fact that she was a good foot taller than him. 'Int Sunday meant for restin?' he asked.

Kay shook her head. 'You remember them free schools backalong, before they started closin?'

'Dunno, weren't much for school myself.'

'Well anyway, this is like them. Religion or no don't mean a thing, this place is all bout business.' The siren sounded and she headed down the incline towards camp and Trey followed.

'Where you bin?' shouted Lamby when he saw Trey return to the yard. 'I bin lookin all over.'

'Went for a walk, what's it to you?'

'You int meant to go off walkin.'

'Who said?'

'It's rules. You'll get into more trouble.'

'I int in trouble.' Trey walked towards the bunkhouse and Lamby followed.

'You are. Got a nicko already, int you? Only trouble-makers get given nickos.'

'Whatever, you got a nickname.'

'That's different.'

'Why?'

'Cus I came with mine. Mum and Dad give it me.'

'You're strange, you know that?'

Lamby grinned suddenly, as though Trey's words were what he wanted to hear.

'You boys comin in or do you want to finish your chatty mothers' meetin first?' DB stood outside Tavy house and when the boys approached he kept to the door frame so they pushed past.

'Comin, sir,' said Lamby.

Trey followed him into the room that had not yet tipped heat from its bowels and he stood with the bristle of sweat about him and looked at his bed by the door.

'That's my bed,' he said to Anders. 'Picked it earlier, put my name down and my clothes and everythin.'

'Tough titty,' said the boy. 'Bin mine for forever.'

'Where's your name then?' asked Trey.

'Don't need to put my name cus everyone knows.'

'Never mind,' grinned Wilder from the bunk beside him. 'We're all brothers together, int we?'

Trey looked down at the reclining boy with his smugness shrink-wrapped and snug around him.

'Where's my clothes?' he asked.

Anders shrugged and looked across at Wilder for affirmation. 'Dunno, look about.' He smiled.

'They're here,' shouted Lamby. 'Good-oh, you're next to me.'

Trey sighed and he went to his bed with all boys watching, waiting for a fight to break out.

'At home I got a double bed, double bed in my own bedroom,' said Lamby.

Trey ignored him.

'Huge bedroom, kitted out with flat-screen TV and everythin, all the game consoles you could think of and all the top games.'

Trey sat down and told Lamby to shut up. He had a headache building and it beat three ways from heat, exertion and stifling fury.

DB ushered the last of the boys into the room and he ordered them to stand at the end of their beds and some boys sniggered and some boys took their time to settle but Trey was learning fast and he stood like a fool in a room full of fools the same.

'It's that time of year again, boys, so if you haven't already I suggest you fill in your forms, medical and next of kin and blah, not that it matters or anythin's changed but it's protocol so do it.'

Trey looked down at Lamby's clipboard at the bottom of his bed. Somebody had written 'Retard' where it asked for medical details and 'King Kong' for his next of kin.

'Is everythin clear?' said DB and he looked at Trey.

'Yes, sir,' said Trey. His voice trembled with anger and sounded like fear.

'Do I make myself clear?'

'Yes, sir,' shouted the other boys.

'Good. Evenin activities are at six tonight cus of the barbecue and all the rest, but usually dinner and prayers is at six and activities seven onwards. You got ten to take a dump or whatever, any questions?'

'When's dinner?' asked Lamby and he put up his hand and asked the question again.

'You got worms, boy? You've just eaten.'

'No, sir, just today, cus of the new boy. Int we only had two meals?'

'God help us.' DB laughed and he turned and left the room.

'I do cards club,' said Lamby and Trey lay on his bed and closed his eyes to ignore him.

'You play?'

'Nope.'

'I can teach you poker if you want.'

'No thanks.'

'We do chemistry,' shouted Anders. 'Chemistry club is the best. We make homebrew but you dint hear it from me.'

'Shut it, Anders,' shouted Wilder. 'Big crackin mouth, you got.'

Trey ignored them all and he took a moment to think about Billy. He wondered what he might be doing at that moment. Cocooned in a hundred blankets and tuck-stuck to a chair not of his choosing, the care home was a different kind of prison. Trey had been there, he'd seen it, a long time ago and briefly, but on some nights he still couldn't wash the smell from his memory.

When the time came for activities he allowed himself to be led by others and he wondered if he might see Kay in passing to help lift his mood.

Activities were nothing much settled into a corner of one big echo of room, a converted outhouse adjacent to the dorms that fell into one of two categories: games or a religious version of schoolwork.

The room was damp and peeling and close to empty and Trey tried his hand at nothing but standing and idling against one of the walls. He kept his eyes fixed on his fiddling fingers and bit at the dry corners of skin and the nowhere nails. From the corner of his eye he could see the idiot boy Lamby set four chairs to a table and sit down to shuffle the deck of cards he was holding.

'Who's up for a game?' he shouted and Trey looked down at his feet. 'Anyone at all?'

'What you playin?' called Wilder.

'Anythin you want,' Lamby wormed up in his seat. 'What you like to play?'

Wilder turned a chair backward and sat down and he told his gang to quit with the sniggering and going on.

'You know a game called "swat the fly"?'

Lamby shook his head.

'You know a game called "spank the tiddler"?'

Lamby attempted to smile. 'You could teach it me?'

Wilder grinned and he looked around the room and his eyes met Trey's.

'How you play it?' asked Lamby.

'What?'

'"Spank the tiddler".'

Everybody laughed.

Wilder took the cards from the boy and he blocked the pack tight to the table. 'It's a game of sharin,' he nodded. 'Everyone gets to play.' He flicked a card at Lamby and then at each of his boys and Trey watched as they fell on to the dirt floor.

'That int a game,' said Lamby.

'Tis. Game int finished yet, we int got to the spankin part.' He stood up and kicked his chair to one side of the room and flipped the table towards the other.

Trey stood free of the wall and he wanted to say something or do something but he told himself that this was not his world for getting into. He left the room with Lamby sitting tiny-tight in the middle of the circling boys and when he passed DB in the corridor he mentioned a fight was about to break out.

'They're just havin a bit of fun,' the man laughed. 'Don't worry bout it, Rudeboy.'

'Just sayin.' Trey shrugged and played it like a no-biggy.

'Lettin off steam is what it is,' DB continued.

'Yes, sir.'

'You gettin an early night?'

'Yes, sir.'

'Good boy, full day tomorrow. Now go on and don't forget to pray.'

Trey nodded a hundred 'yes, sirs'.

He walked to the bunkhouse with his feet kicking and tailing, the good and the bad at war within. He wished he were stronger and he wished he were less of a chicken and he wished he was someone else. If he was he would have stuck up for the boy. He thought about the choices made in life and the little choices made in passing, and right and wrong were muddied in everything did, done and said.

Inside the bunkhouse he sat on his bed in a fidget and he picked at his hands and picked at his head until the scrabbling demon was dug from out of hiding. Tomorrow he would play himself into a better light and start the search for the man he knew was his parents' killer.

He sat back and dangled his legs from off the side of the bed and was about to lie back when he saw the chaplain standing at the door.

'Tremain.' He smiled.

'Yes, sir.' Trey sat up and then he stood.

'No need for ceremony, sit down.' He stepped once into the room and continued to smile.

'So how you gettin on? First day and all that.'

Trey shrugged. 'OK, sir.'

'And you int had no problems settlin and whatever?'

'No, sir.' Trey felt uneasy. He liked it better when adults were strict.

'Just tired, sir,' he added.

'Good, well if you have any problems, anythin at all then don't hesitate to come find me. I'm master of Lynner house.'

Trey nodded. He knew that already.

'What bout em others?' he asked.

'Tavy is DB, which obviously you know, and Tamar is McKenzie.'

'What bout the other one?'

'Plym? That's the Preacher, but he don't need to spend much time cus that's the older boys, and they known the Preacher long enough to behave. Anyway, any problems let me know.'

Trey watched the man leave and then he wondered about him and all the house masters and wished there was something more certain in his memory so that he might recognise his parents' killer. He kept losing the thread of what it was he was trying to do. It was meant to be so simple, but each man in camp settled somewhere between maybe, maybe not. DB was too short, the chaplain too gentle, and no matter how he wished it was McKenzie who'd killed his parents something about his voice and manner wasn't right. There was a part of him that wished he knew how to accept defeat, but the demon wouldn't have it and while he waited for the others to return Trey went back to that fateful morning and like a movie stuck on a loop he played it out all over again.

'What's up with you?' asked Lamby as he limped towards him.

'What's up with you the same?' Trey settled casual and uncaring on the bed.

'Nothin.'

'Why you limpin?'

'Nothin, just a bit of messin. It's all good.'

Trey shook his head and he looked across at the glut of bully boys coming through the door and some nodded and he nodded back.

'You like activities?' asked Lamby.

'What was there to like?'

He lay back fully and hoped the boy wasn't one for going on through the night and he told him he was dead dog tired. The light went out and there was a brief moment of tranquillity. Trey gazed up at the smudge of night sky through the one grimy skylight in the tin roof above. He thought about the boy in the bed next to him and shame came crashing in a stomp through the dorm.

Across the room Wilder and his gang were strik-ing matches and throwing them at each other and he watched the beautiful flights of flame as they rocketed through the tepid gloom and part of him hoped they'd set the beds alight for the magnificence of fire.

The heat in the place was like a pyre and Trey untangled himself from his sheets and lay cooling until condensation gathered beneath the metal ceiling above and spat occasional dribble-drops down upon his chest.

He glanced about the room for the all-clear and stretched to take the photo from the back pocket of his floor-flung jeans. He needed to set things back on firmer ground like he did every night before he went to sleep.

He leant on his side with the photo tipped from view and slowed his breathing down to seaside thinking. The tiny cut of blue sky he stretched out and pinned beyond the four corners of its paper frame and the thin line of ocean he let flood and he closed his eyes as it pulled him under. Mum and Dad holding him in the swing of things and Billy threatening to dip him under, everybody laughing, best day last day ever after.

With memories made mighty he slipped the photo beneath his pillow and whispered the goodnights like he did every night and when Lamby asked him what he was mumbling he told him nothing and to mind his own.

'Only if it's bout the rain don't mind it.'

'What you talkin bout?' asked Trey.

'The rain above, you get used to it; spose you do anyway.'

Trey pulled the sheet up over his head. 'Like most things,' he said.

'Like everythin,' the boy answered.

CHAPTER THREE

Trey woke to the sound of the strange boy talking through a wardrobe dilemma. Would he wear his T-shirt or would he wear his vest? Trey turned into the rough-mesh pillow and tried to retrieve what was left of an OK dream, a dream that didn't involve fight and fire and fear, but it had abandoned him.

Trey sighed and he turned and looked about the dimly lit room, one solitary light bulb swung worn and cleaved with dust, a nothing light.

'Why they bother with the light in the mornin?' he asked and he looked up at the cracked window above the door and saw that it was going to be another hot day.

'Int got no choice,' said Lamby. 'It's set on a timer.'

'Why don't someone open the door?'

'Still locked.' He came close and bent his face into view. 'You excited?'

'Bout what?'

50

'Today, your first full day in camp. The first full day's the best day, I'd say.'

Trey sighed.

'What?'

'I knew you'd say somethin like that.'

'And I did!' The boy squealed and he opted for the T-shirt.

When the siren boomed into the room Trey dressed quick and went to stand at the door and he ignored the jabbing Wilder and waited for it to be unlocked.

'You're eager,' the boy said from his bunk by the door.

'Just want some fresh air,' said Trey. 'Stinks in here.'

'Int so bad.'

Trey shrugged and the demon inside kicked at the ground, confusion circling and boiling because Wilder was hard to read.

'Gonna tell us a bit bout yourself, Rudeboy? You and me got a fair bit in common, I reckon.'

Trey tried the door despite knowing it was locked. The claustrophobia that was forever in him was threatening to rear and his hands were near to scratching the walls.

'What's there to tell?' he asked.

'I dunno.' Wilder slid to his feet and he stood against the wall next to Trey. 'Give us a piece of yourself, see if we wanna let you click up.'

Trey gripped his hands into his pockets to keep the monster that was demon down. He just wanted to get gone. 'Who says I wanna join your gang?' he asked and it was the demon talking. The demon who poked at him with talons and threatened to bust from the inside out.

'What you say to me?' Wilder came close.

'I int got no problem with you. Just keep myself to myself, that's all.'

Wilder laughed wet into his face and he snapped thumb and finger towards his gang and they laughed too.

'We got ourselves a lone wolf here, boys. Broodin bubble of a boy by all accounts.'

Trey wanted to add something in his defence but the intimidation had him pebble small. When the door swung open he pushed through with the other waiting boys.

'You in a rush, int you?' DB shouted as he bolted past but Trey ignored him and went to find a spot for sitting and collecting thoughts away from other kids.

Trey knew Wilder was angling some version of friendship towards him and he didn't want it and more than that he didn't want to have to say that he didn't want it. There was nothing wrong with liking solitude when you were a loner; it was a used-to thing and a right thing and better for all concerned.

When his mind returned to the day of the fire he took solace in it and settled down to thinking time. He remembered lying in the bed in the room that was supposedly his, a room shared with other boys that passed through the home like eels through a net. Trey had been passed around from foster home to foster home since the day he was found out on the cliffs and taken into care. He really was a lone wolf. He had no family other than those in the ground and Billy, who had been reduced to child in one momentary blast and then hidden away like a shameful secret. Trey had no friends either and there lay a billion reasons too complicated.

Other kids didn't like him. He was too quiet and he didn't like to fight but when he did he'd fight too much. He'd get into trouble when the demon fire came to his head and then into his hands. Pyro-boy, they called him and, he had to admit, he liked that bit.

The plan started as a little germ thing tickling, an itch thing he knew he had to scratch in order to get wrong-sided with the law. Trey knew about the camp the same way all kids knew about it when the first fence went up two years back. It was on the TV and the radio and in the newspaper that wrapped his chips on a Friday. The place that all the bad kids got put and the only place in Cornwall for a boy like Trey: Camp Kernow. The place where his parents' killer got to rule over the kids with an iron rod. Talk in the towns and villages was never far from speculation about the camp good and bad, but when he overheard a conversation between his foster carers and a community policeman, he knew who it was they were talking about.

Trey remembered sitting outside on the back step, the kitchen window swung wide because of the warm spring weather and the adults talking freely, gossiping the way they did when they thought kids weren't around. At first it was just chat and words and whatever. Trey was waiting for them to take their coffee into the front room so he could steal a cigarette from the carton on the top of the cabinet and he whispered for them to hurry up and he played impatiently with his lighter.

Sitting there now in camp he couldn't recall when the conversation that was nothing more than idle chalk-dust talk became flint-thrown words. He couldn't remember the exact moment when he heard the head-lines that made up the story of his life: coastal village, double murder, killer never found. It was a story that had no memory of the poor orphan kids and that was one thing in Trey's favour, that and the words he heard next: Camp Kernow, safe haven for the murderer.

It was enough to start him wondering, but, when he read in the local paper about the camp that taught hard work and Christian values to the wayward, wonder was replaced by fact. The group photo of the masters and the Preacher all smiles with a bundle of kids under each of their arms; Trey knew this was his destiny.

He worked his idea into a job-done plan and he marked the day when everyone was out working or scallying or whatever. An early summer morning with a calm smile slapped straight across it, an unsuspecting good old-fashioned country day. It was a Friday; the others would have the weekend to sort things out in the aftermath.

The fire part was the easy part. Cans of red diesel stored in a barn were all Trey needed for the job and he was mindful to catch every corner of every room with the spill.

He remembered the smell like it was sweet-shop heaven sent. The diesel and then the flick-clip flame and the deep-heat Taser tang that fizzed his taste buds and peeled his nostrils wide.

It took everything in him not to stand too close to the rising pyre, be taken in by his own handiwork, his might.

He stood outside with his bag of silly sentimental things, the one good photo and the only photo of his family gripped firm in his fist and Dad's watch double tight on his wrist, waiting for the sirens and the scolding, waiting for the cleansing that followed destruction.

Trey knew his future lay in the heat of those attention-grabbing flames, but it also existed in the cool, slow rising ashes.

When the sun pushed close he tucked himself into a thin wedge of shade and his thoughts wandered towards Kay and he looked over at the girls' dorm. Just to see her from afar would have been something to lift his spirit.

She wasn't a push-shove kid like the rest of them; she was built of stronger stuff, there was detail in her lining, her fabric, and Trey knew he could learn from that.

He stubbed his toes and made patterns in the sandy earth and when he saw Lamby heading his way he dug his eyes into the ground. Something in him rattled with guilt for not standing up for the lad yesterday and he supposed he wanted to apologise, shame was he didn't know how.

'Howdy, partner,' the boy grinned. 'Wondered where you'd got to.' He blocked Trey's view and put his hands on his hips. 'Well?' he asked.

'Well what?'

'Where'd you get to?'

'Here.'

'Here what?'

'I got to here, sittin here.'

'You int comin for breakfast? You'll get more'n you ask for at breakfast.'

'Really?' Trey stood up and stretched. 'Like what?' His stomach started to grumble.

'Prayers.'

Trey sighed. 'Not again.'

'You're funny. Int you noticed were stuck behind sacred bars?'

'Fence.'

'What's that?'

'We're stuck behind a fence. So where we eat anyway?'

'Dint you see that old circus tent when you arrived?'

'The marquee?'

'Whatever you wanna call it, that's the food tent.'

They walked towards the tent and Lamby told Trey about the chaplain that gave morning prayer.

'He's a good old boy by all accounts. Bit quirko but int we all.'

'I met him.'

'You did?'

'Yesterday, int he to do with pastoral or whatever they call it?'

'Spose. Bit of a pushover but he means well, more'n others, he does.'

They entered the tent and sat on benches where told and Trey watched the others get filed and pushed the same.

'Don't the Preacher give the prayers?' Trey asked.

'Course not.'

'Ever?'

'Never, he's too busy runnin things.'

'What things?'

'Jeez, questions.'

'Just askin.'

'He's the head of the church, the boss. Don't worry, you'll probably never meet him.'

Trey sat with his back hunched against the canvas wall and he closed his eyes to shut in the confusing anger and he listened to the racing wind outside. He felt it claw at his shoulder blades and finger his ribs and he leant into it to feel its power.

The sudden thought that he might never find his parents' killer had him burn bush-fire wild. Naively, he had thought revenge would be exacted in three easy steps: find the man, kill the man and escape. He hadn't spent much time working out the detail of step two and three, but here he was stumped at the first.

He put his knees up to his chest and held them close. The chaplain was storming on in regards to good and evil and Trey wondered what he knew from experience and what he'd trawled up from the Bible. He looked around and saw most of the other kids shuffling and picking at themselves and he looked down at his hands and realised he was doing the same.

He wondered about time and his watch that had been taken and he dug his thumb into the soft split of sinew and flesh where it should have been and felt his heart beat demon blood.

He looked at the wrists of other boys and girls that sat close and nothing but scars on scars circled there. Even time had been sanctioned, another thing taken.

'They've stolen time,' he whispered to Lamby.

'What?'

'Time, they've taken it.'

Lamby leant forward and put his hand to Trey's head. 'You feelin all right?'

'Course.'

'Int got one of your headaches or such?'

'Shut up, just sayin. Nobody got a watch on.'

'That's cus they've been taken off us.'

'So how we sposed to know the time?'

'We int.'

Trey waited for the chaplain to reach whatever point he was trying to make and when he climaxed some of the younger kids laughed but most of the older ones looked blankly on. He eyed the two house masters lodged either side of the tent, and he thought about the chaplain and Preacher too, and he imagined a roulette wheel spinning with their collective crimes.

It was a known thing that the men who worked the juvenile camps had criminal records themselves. Religion had saved those men the same way it would save the kids, this was their mantra, and Trey supposed some believed it; it helped relieve the symptoms of sin. The way things were heading on the outside, sin played a bigger, better game than that of what was known as good. You did right by God and law and all and nothing returned to you except poverty. This was how Trey saw it and those who were just like him saw it; both weathered and dog-dead tired they were sick to their gums of living hand to mouth. The rich got richer in their charge for power and all the while the poor fell to the gutter, left to scratch out some replication of happy living in the subsistent village ghettos.

This was how it was in the country and Trey supposed this was how it was in the towns and cities the land over.

When the preaching and the propagandising were complete and all souls supposedly saved they lined up for an unremarkable loose-meat sandwich and they stood outside in the stripping wind and awaited instructions while they ate.

The sun was a monstrous heartbeat in the sky and it pounded out its rhythm throughout the compound.

'Why we waitin round?' asked Trey. 'Can't we just go do what we're sposed to do?' Trey went to look inside his sandwich and then thought better of it.

'They love to boss us just for the sake of bossin. You probs won't be workin today anyway.'

'Why not?'

'You gotta do tests,' said Lamby. 'They gotta test you and stuff.'

'Like what?'

'Stuff.'

'Stuff like what?'

'I dunno. Don't worry, it's just profilin, work out if you're mad, not mad etc.'

'What are you?'

'Me? I'm defo mad, but then they knew that before I got here. I got a record for madness goin way back.' He started to grin and Trey edged away slightly.

'He's harmless,' said Kay from behind. 'Harmless enough anyway.'

'I int harmless,' Lamby protested. 'Could go mental mad if I wanted to.'

'Whatever, come on we gotta go.' She grabbed Lamby by the arm and Trey watched them disappear into the crowd and he wished he was going with them.

'Rudeboy,' shouted McKenzie suddenly. 'Get over here.'

Trey looked around him and he watched the crowd disperse before kicking forward.

'Looks like it's just you and me, boy,' he smiled. 'Today we're gonna have a little fun, do some iddy-biddy tests to sort the wheat from the chaff. How bout it?'

Trey nodded.

'How bout it, Rudeboy?'

'Yes, sir.'

'Yes, sir, indeed.'

McKenzie went to the office upstairs in Tamar house where he was master and Trey followed and he sat at the table across from him. If he was going to swing the good-boy routine he had to jump through every hoop that reeled his way. Trey knew McKenzie was a tough old bastard. Men like him were always found prowling the dark corners and corridors of care homes and detention centres. They were drawn to juveniles and vulnerables through their love of inflicting fear. McKenzie was a man who was all about intimidation; he wasn't like DB, who Trey had noticed took bribes from certain soft-centred boys, let them off the hook for his own secret delight.

Trey wanted to show McKenzie that he wasn't stupid and he proved this by deducing the shape and shift of the grilling and all morning he wheeled out the answers the man wanted to hear.

Yes to the regrets and yes to learning from his mistakes and yes, yes, yes to the everything that meant he would be left alone. Those in charge thought they had him folded, a neat square boy ready to slip into the Preacher's pocket. He signed the contract of promises and he went to the medical office that was situated at the rear of the shower block to be poked and pulled and prodded by some struck-off sunk-drunk doctor and everything about him gave green light. He was fit for physical duty, same as every dumb-ass criminal kid.

Outside the medical room Trey took his time to return his papers to McKenzie's office and he made his way towards the yard. An argument had broken out between two girls and he stood in the shadow of the bunkhouses to watch and he settled himself out of the wind and waited for the punches to fly with the other circling kids.

'You took your time,' said McKenzie when he finally returned to the office.

Trey passed him the papers. 'Yes, sir,' he said.

'Any reason? Cus breaktime don't mean your breaktime.'

'No, sir.' Trey shrugged. 'Sorry, sir.' He thought to say something about the fight and then thought better of it and instead he stood in front of the master and awaited instructions.

'We need to work out how clever you are, Rudeboy, see if you got a brain rattlin round that skull of yours.'

'Yes, sir.' Trey sat down and he rested the papers on the desktop in front of him and McKenzie sat opposite, his back turned and his boots slammed one two against the window frame.

Trey liked the seriousness of tests and the order that played there was akin to showing off, a bit of spark that fired from him like fireworks. Dad said he was a bright spark, told him this over when he was a knee-high boy, told him to get-up and get-on no matter how hard he cried. Mum said he didn't mean to be tough, but it was all right; Trey knew it was all for the good. Trey was the first to walk out of all the kids in the village, Dad said, the first to talk too. 'Billy' was his first word; that boy was on his mind right from the start. He supposed he could have made something of learning if it hadn't been for the circumstances that put the demon into his head and the fire into his hands. It was too late now; things that had been lost in his parents' passing were lost for good.

Trey answered the questions and ticked the choice boxes in record time and when he had finished he allowed himself a moment of silent sitting and then he said that he was done for the impression it might make.

Trey waited for McKenzie to turn and he watched his head list slightly and he realised he was napping. He said his name again and he looked about the poky room and at the pen in his hand and he twiddled it through his fingers and wondered how hard it would be to take one man down and he agreed that it would be easy and he said it out loud and the demon agreed.

'What's that?' asked McKenzie, waking and turning in his seat.

'Finished, sir.' Trey got up and put the papers and the pen in front of him.

'What you want, a trophy?'

'No, sir.'

'Well then do one, I'm busy.'

'Yes, sir.' He left McKenzie's office and wondered what was meant next and he watched the door swing closed and lock behind him and he moved into the shade to think.

With break over the main area of the camp had emptied of all living souls and Trey could not have felt more alone. He put himself into the white-light day when the shade was sucked out of hiding and he circled the yard and passed the slaughter buildings and he kept on walking out on to the arid moor with the buzz in his head that came from a thousand thoughts and not one good.

Away from the rattling steel dormitory buildings he found a small granite quarry in which to sit and he settled between the shards of rust-rot machinery and what wasn't set as deathtrap and rested his head. If there was another way to thinking that didn't involve scarper then he would have done it but there wasn't. He had an excuse in any case, he hadn't been given orders and Trey was used to a life of remit.

He thought about Billy and wished him close for the chat no matter how one-sided and he thought about Mum and Dad and both were in the same place of happy. There was something in the paddling-pool circle of water at the centre of the quarry that stopped all the worry inside and he went down to the tiny make-believe shore and crouched like a giant beside it and he waited. Daydream time moved quickly and it reduced Trey down to a boy sea-sand sitting. He made a boat from some dry-leaf drifting and splinter-wood needled within and he set it sail with a reckoning that Dad would have approved of its design.

Dad was all about the boats and fishing. Nothing much had mattered more than the rig and a smooth ocean ride. He could catch anything. Trey had been there forever times when all the boats came into the harbour with their catch, Billy too. Billy was a natural when it came to fishing, Dad said he had it in him. Maybe his brother still did, Trey hoped so.

Trey sailed his boat out into the mucky puddle ocean and he blew it shore to shore with the imaginary chat going off in his head. Once more he was that boy before he had got lost in the shoot of things. Fifteen nearly sixteen and playing in the dust and the dirt and a puddle.

He wondered what Mum and Dad would think of him now; a good boy, bad boy, strange boy. Getting into trouble like always as a kid, he never meant things to go wrong but just about everything he said or did turned up rotten, always taking the rap for all the stupid sillies.

He thought about love and the guidance that came tied to it and tried to bury the thoughts that settled towards his brother. If he closed his eyes he could still picture him in the nursing home that one beat-stop time he was allowed to visit, a rootless young man with his short life spent shuffling from one end of a corridor to the other. A subsiding chasm stretched between life and death. He was a dead man walking in old man slippers. Trey didn't like the image he had of him there, he wanted him in that boat, fishing.

The daydream could have drifted on into the dark and Trey would have waited for the moon and stars to surround him and he would have built Dad and Billy a bit-stick fire on the shore if it wasn't for sudden voices. The hook surprise of reality's pull had his lungs fight for air and his heart leap from his chest and he flattened to the ground and crawled to the scatter of metal junk.

When the boom of blood left his ears he listened and he waited until what was there then wasn't. A door scraped open and slammed shut and it took away the voices somewhere below ground until whispers and silence and gone.

Trey stood and he climbed to the ridge of the quarry and he saw for the first time the door hidden flush in the arid land like a trap. He went to it and put his ear to listen for the men but they were long gone swallowed and he sat beside it in the hope that it might give something of itself. Another thing to think about and, when the end of activities siren went off, the discovery of the trapdoor was another thing to worry about too.

Back in the bunkhouse he lay on his bed with the stretch of hunger in his gut and he filtered what information he had about the camp into jars of possibility.

'Dint see you at supper,' said Lamby. 'Sunday supper's the best. You do somethin bad to keep you back?'

Trey sighed and told him to be quiet, he was thinking.

'Thinkin what?'

'Stuff.'

'What stuff?'

'Personal stuff. Shut it, would you?'

'Charmin.'

'Whatever.'

'Why dint you go to supper?'

'I was busy.'

'Busy how?'

Trey sat up and stared at him and Lamby sat down quickly.

'Don't hit me, I was just askin. I saved you a couple of roasties.'

'I int gonna hit you.' Trey took the potatoes and thanked him.

'Good spuds, int they?'

Trey nodded and thanked him over.

'So how'd the tests go?'

'OK.'

'No skeletons in your mental closet?'

'Only the ones I know bout.'

'What bout the ones you don't know bout?'

'Them int worth nothin.'

'You sure? Cus I got things I don't know bout in my mental closet that are off the scale.'

'How you know if you don't know?'

'Cus I bin told, stupo. You ask some dumbos, don't you?'

Trey shook his head. The crazy boy really was crazy after all.

'Is that why you in here?' he asked. 'Cus you're mental?'

Lamby shrugged. 'Spose, it's not good to pick over the bones too closely. Some say you should analyse everythin, but you shouldn't.'

'Why not?'

'In case you don't like what you find, then ...'

Trey pushed back against the wall and he had to admit the crazy boy talked more sense than most.

'Go on.'

'Once you picked over your life and all the rights and wrongs, what you got left?'

'Is that a question?'

'Tis.'

Trey shrugged. 'I dunno.'

'A big pile of bones and you don't know what goes where and you don't know up from down.' He moved across to sit on Trey's bed and Trey surprised himself by letting him.

'What I'm sayin is, you gotta remember that you got a whole lot of crap in a pot noosed round your neck, but you don't wanna look into that pot too closely.'

'Cus you know you int gonna like what you see?'

'There is that and somethin else.'

'What?'

'It stinks.'

They both laughed and Trey wanted to say something friendly to the boy but a lifetime of resistance had him tongue-tied.

'Anyway,' he said, 'I spose I should say sorry bout last night.' He fumbled his fingers in a panic to find something to chew.

'What bout last night?'

'Leavin you to the dogs. Wilder and that.'

'Wilder? I int bothered bout him. I got bigger burgers to flip than Wilder.'

Trey looked at Lamby and he wondered if this was swagger talk. 'But he smacked you, dint he?' he asked.

'Yeah, spose he did, but he can't hurt me inside, can he? He can try but it int happenin.'

The siren rang out the ten-minute warning and Trey told Lamby to get the hell off his bunk before the light went off.

'Don't worry, I int plannin on snugglin or nothin.'

'Well that's good to hear.' Trey pulled the sheet up around him and the two boys settled down to the sound of the other boys' banter for sanctuary's sake.

'And, Trey?'

'What?'

'Apology accepted.'

'It weren't an apology, I was just sayin.'

'Well thank you for just sayin.'

Trey turned into the wall and he sailed himself to sleep with the good and the bad and a million disconcerting questions. No matter what the boy said about Wilder something was bubbling beneath.

CHAPTER FOUR

Early Monday morning and Trey stood beneath the tepid splash of water and he closed his eyes to shut out the horror that was the sight of naked boys. He knew McKenzie and DB were standing at the shower-block door and it unnerved him to think of their slow eyes slipping and sliding over them like they were prey.

He turned his back to the door and was quick with the soap and rinse and he ran to his towel with the demon dying inside.

In the changing rooms he stood in the corner to towel dry and he ignored Wilder's torrent of questions until his jeans were firmly in place.

'So you play sports or no?' the boy asked.

'Why?'

'Touchy lad, int you? Just bein friendly.'

Trey put on his vest and stretched it a little to make it fit. 'Spose I lifted weights a bit in young offenders.'

'You had a gym?'

'Just in the yard.' He sat on a bench to put on his socks and trainers and Wilder sat next to him.

'You miss the place?'

Trey wondered what the boy was aiming at. 'Not really, I weren't there for long, the usual two-week assessment to see where to put me, if I should stay there or be sent here.'

'And they decided to send you here, must be a real hard nut. What you do?'

'Arson. I don't mind. Get more freedom here with the open air and that.'

Wilder laughed. 'Is that how they sold it you?'

'What you mean?'

'Bet they told you this place was a half-step to leadin a normal life.'

Trey ignored him and stood up.

'They did, dint they? That's the problem with you newbies, so damn gullible.'

'I int no newbie to all of this, I know how the system works.'

'Not this one, mate. I got inside information, you'll see. They rollin these hard-ass places out all over the country. Camps are cheaper'n young offenders. Government thinks it's got it all worked out sellin em on to private companies.'

Trey shrugged. He just wanted to get away.

'Slave labour,' the boy continued.

'What you mean?' Trey asked.

'Cheap labour, learn a trade, my hole. 'Cept me of course, I'm learnin the family business.'

Trey ignored him but when Wilder stood close he realised the conversation was not yet over. 'What's that?' he asked.

The boy tapped his nose and said secrets were secrets.

Other boys filed into the changing room and Trey spied an escape route away from Wilder and he took it. He stood outside and found a place downwind of the acrid smoke that plagued the camp night and day and he looked across the yard towards the bunkhouses. Despite his best efforts a little of Kay's beauty had been lost to him in the night and he couldn't wait to see her. He leant against the tin-bump wall and put his hands into his pockets and felt for his lighter to know it was there. Security came in knowing that he was a flick away from warmth of his choosing. A spark to turn his life from useless tinder into something more and that single thought felt good.

He watched the sun sluice sudden heat into every corner of the camp and it shrank the black shadow squares into dazzling white. He stepped from the thin strip of shade and out into the heat and turned his face to the good morning buzz.

No matter what Wilder or anyone else said, he was no newbie. Standing smack bang in the centre of camp without anyone knowing his true reason was enough, it was all something. He was a sniff away from revenge and freeing his brother. In two months' time he would turn sixteen, he'd be able to get a job and find some derelict shack to do up, a sweet home from home down by the sea. He'd look out for Billy the way as kids he looked out for him. It could work, it would work, it had to. Trey smiled at the idea of a simple life and he stood happy in thought until the others came into the yard.

Together they loped towards the dining tent and Trey fell in with the standing and idling in line and he took up a bowl and spoon and waited for the one thick slap of porridge.

'Where's the sugar?' he asked the boy serving.

'Already comes with.'

'Where?'

'It's in it, stupid.'

Trey took a poke and a lick with his finger. 'Tastes more like salt.'

'Well it int. What you want, fancy syrup?'

'Salt's what they have in Scotland,' said Lamby jumping in beside him. 'That's their preference.'

Trey saw him try to think of a way to shorten the word and he told him not to bother.

'Anyway, there's ways to gettin sugar on the black market in this place.'

'Wilder runs it, no doubt,' said Trey.

'Guess so.'

'Spose he's got money cus of his dad or whatever?'

They carried their bowls to a table that was not yet occupied. 'Don't dis him, not in public anyway.'

'Why not?' asked Trey as they sat down. 'I int in any case.'

'Cus I don't reckon his dad is no bigo businessman like he makes out. Bit of a rough-around himself I'd say. Don't say nothin, poor kid's in denial.'

'That's why he beats you,' said Trey. 'Cus you got somethin on him.'

Lamby shrugged. 'Maybe, maybe not, I'm working on it.'

They sat silent and mouthed grace when it was asked of them and Trey dipped his head obediently with the blah going off in his mouth despite his mind talking otherwise.

With grace over he sat forward and ate the salt-grit porridge with a grimace and he wondered which of the two boys was the bigger liar. There was something not quite right about Wilder but Lamby was roundabout the same. There was a reason Trey didn't trust anyone; people were just plain untrustworthy.

He sat with his eyes on the lookout for Kay and when a trolley of tea and hot squash wheeled past he asked for one of each and poured the tea into the porridge and drank it down.

'You're a weirdo,' smiled Lamby. 'Defo.'

'You like eatin this stuff?'

'Spose. Just food, init?'

'Barely.'

'Tastes OK to me.'

'Well don't that make you the weirdo?'

Lamby laughed and for the second time Trey kind of liked him despite the mistrust and he supposed it was nice to have someone for the idling.

He held the hot orange in both hands and wished he had a cigarette to go with it and Lamby said there were ways for getting that too.

'Well I'm gonna have to find the ways.'

'See if you int got somethin to trade,' said Lamby.

Trey shrugged. 'Like what?'

'I dunno; you got to work out what it is someone might want. Keep swappin till you get the thing that the kid that got the fags wants.'

Trey watched Kay stand in line and wait for her bowl to be filled and he felt something inside him rip and break and build back wrong. He took a gulp of the orange drink and despite its heat he swallowed. He saw Lamby watching him and he coughed and asked what he had on Kay.

'Best you don't know.'

'Know what?'

'Best you don't ask the same.'

'You know why she's in here or no?'

'Bit. Don't go askin though. She don't like folks askin.'

Kay spun her metal bowl on to the table and sat across from the boys.

'Mornin,' she nodded, chewing the spoon.

'Mornin, Kayo.' Lamby grinned and winked at Trey.

'Rule number one, please don't call me that, it's way too early for that.'

Trey smiled. 'He's got a word for everythin just about.'

Kay nodded. 'And I got a name for him.'

'Larry,' laughed Lamby.

'Idiot.' She shook her head at the thick porridge before splitting it with the spoon and Trey watched her.

'So you workin with me today or no?' she asked, not bothered either way.

Trey shrugged. 'Don't know, I think so.' He wanted to say more but the shy thing had his tongue twisted.

'I'll go ask,' said Lamby and he jumped to his feet and went to the area reserved for the chaplain and the house masters.

'He's an odd one, he is.' Trey put a foot up on the bench for some style of cool.

'He's got his reasons.'

'You know him long?'

'I known everyone long. He's a good lad, an idiot but a good un.'

'He likes you I'd say, as friends I mean.' Trey felt the cool inside him melt and pool. 'Not that there's anythin wrong with likin you another way.' The heat came to his cheeks and he looked away.

Kay laughed and carried on eating and Trey knew that she knew he liked her in that way. Of course she did. Just about every boy in the place must like her in that way.

He saw Lamby creep about the masters and he watched them for hidden signs and codes. He could see their mouths tighten with amusement and he looked at their wagging hands and searched them for signs of unwashable blood, the crud and stain of slaughter. Trey bit at his fingernails and wished for one solitary clue that would lead him to the killer.

'Yep you're with us,' said Lamby when he returned to the table. 'I said you dint want to do farmin just to be sure. Reverse psycho, it's called.'

They all laughed and Trey stubbed a bit of blood on to his jeans.

'So what you got planned for us today, boss?' Lamby asked Kay.

'Rule number two, do not call me that.' She turned to Trey. 'He thinks I like it, I don't.'

With breakfast shovelled and swallowed Trey followed the others across the compound towards the farm and when they passed two idling boys Kay said they worked farm too.

Trey nodded towards them and the lads who were twins nodded back.

'This is John and David.' Kay shouted over her shoulder. 'They're identical if you dint know.' She looked back at Trey and smiled.

'I'm Trey,' he said, looking up at the boys. 'I seen you bout camp.'

'This here's John,' said Lamby and he linked arms with the boy who towered over him. 'And that there is David. They're mute so don't bother waitin for no chat. Them what you call strong silent types. Not like me, I'm weak as a twig.'

They passed the farm barn and carried on towards the part of camp that was meant for rearing cattle, a group of fields that settled at the opposite end of the compound, and was high and far enough to give the impression that it had somehow liberated itself from the confines of captivity. Field upon field it stretched itself along the edge of the fence and where granite pushed from the earth it pushed back; pasture green and yellow from the first cut of summer.

Kay told him one lone thing worth knowing about the cows was to not get attached and Trey had guessed that already. 'Them's for eatin and nothin more and that's a shame but there int nothin we can do bout it.'

Trey looked over the wooden gate towards the animals grazing on sugar beet in the far corner of one of the fields and he wondered if they had any sense of destiny. The electrocution and the chop and the table, the intimacy of blood and death had him tipped wrong. It was everywhere; he could smell it.

'Today we got trenches,' Kay continued. 'Masters said we got trenches all week so that's what we got.' She pointed at a belly roll of untouched land beyond the barns and told the twins to go load the pickup with axes and shovels.

'You two can come with me.' She jumped over the gate and into the field and Trey and Lamby followed.

'What's with all the fences?' asked Trey.

'Keeps things in,' said Lamby. 'Keeps the cattle in for one.'

'What bout the trenches?'

'We dig em and then they put storage units over em.'

'Why?'

Lamby shook his head. 'Can't tell you.'

'You know but can't tell or you can't tell cus you don't know?'

Lamby stopped for a second. 'The first one,' he said.

'You know much bout any of the masters?' Trey asked.

'Not much, why would I?'

'You bin here long enough.'

'So?'

'So what you know bout the Preacher?'

Lamby shook his head.

'What?'

'Won't do to ask bout the boss.'

'Why not?'

'Just cus. Don't you wanna know bout the cows? What breed and whatever else?'

Trey sighed. 'What bout em?'

'They're called limousine and they can be moody beasts so don't have a go at em or they'll have a go at you back. I guess you could say they're sensitive.'

'I don't blame em with what fate got planned,' said Kay.

'What you feed em?' asked Trey.

'We got silage to give em whenever and hay in winter. But don't give just anythin, ask me first.'

Trey wanted to ask more questions to keep her talking but he knew Lamby was watching him. 'What?' he asked.

'So what you in for anyway?' the boy asked. 'You askin questions bout all else, I'm in for armed robbery.'

'What you rob?' Trey asked. He already had the boy marked as a joker.

'Village post office. Only I wasn't really a part of the robbery, just happened to be there when it went down, then I kind of went along for the ride in the getaway car, then ta-da.'

'Ta-da what?'

'Whad'ya know, I'm doin time.'

Trey studied him closely, watched his smile pull and ping like a snapper-band tightening.

'Mum and Dad weren't too pleased. Pride and joy and all that.'

'You like it here?' asked Trey. 'Seems you do.'

'It's all right, much the same as home in many ways.'

'Like what?'

'Just ways.' Lamby realised that Kay had continued walking and he called out for her to wait and she stood angled and cross.

'What?' she shouted, her hands were muddy and she wiped them on her jeans.

'I'm givin Trey some backstory, fillin him in.'

Trey could see she was trying not to smile, her dark eyes sparking within the forever outdoor tan.

'Not my fault everyone else is borin, got to fill the gaps with my own this and that. You gonna tell me why you're in?'

'Nope.'

'I told you mine.'

'So? Dint mean I wanted to hear it.'

'Moody type, int you? A right mystery.'

'Not used to chattin,' said Trey and they followed Kay through the uncultivated fields and stopped when she stopped.

'Why you wanna know bout the masters anyway?'

'I don't.'

'Do too. Trey wants to know bout the masters,' he shouted towards Kay, 'and the Preacher.'

'No I don't.' Trey kicked at the ground and he warned the demon to keep his tongue zipped in his teeth if he wanted to stay in the shadows. Questions had to be stored deep in the shovelled ground until the time was right for digging.

'What we got here?' asked Lamby suddenly.

'Broken fence.' Kay kicked at a partially rotten post and it fell back on to the ground. 'Rotten through, we'll have to replace it before the cows get to it.'

Trey helped Lamby take down the rotten posts and Kay unpicked the wire with the pocket knife she kept sharp and hidden in a slip of leather in her boot.

When the twins arrived they unloaded everything useful from the truck and Trey and Lamby sat on the flat-bed and watched the others bash new posts into place with the driver and secure a run of wire with loop nails.

'So you got anythin worthy to tell me at all?' asked Lamby.

Trey looked across at the boy and shrugged. 'Spose not.'

'Don't trust me enough to tell me nothin, is that it?'

'Don't have nothin to tell.'

Lamby nodded his head knowingly. 'I know you do, just a matter of time till you tell me. Don't worry, I can wait.'

'You two plannin on sittin there all day?' shouted Kay and Trey was glad to escape the grilling.

'You int said what we're meant to do,' said Lamby.

'Trenches,' said Trey. 'Where we meant to dig?'

Kay pointed towards the far end of the fence. 'Take a pickaxe and spade each, it's marked out on the ground. We'll stay here and fix the fence.'

The two boys made their way across the side curve of moor and Trey felt a bit of mood scratching inside him.

He felt good and he felt bad all in a mix. He didn't like crowds, but neither did he like worming one-to-ones.

They found the slap of land with string staked in squares to the ground and Trey took to digging with a good full-pump hit of hope and hate in his heart. The sun was already slamming hot in the sky and its heat split the earth with a bang. He shouldered the pickaxe and swung it with an eye to the fractal cracked land and sometimes he aimed it just right and sometimes it missed and sent flashes of silver dust up into his face. He thought about the long hot summer laid out in the immediate future and he thought about forever summers in the long gone past.

He wished he'd paid more attention to the stop-clock minutes of his short life, filed memories into storage for later, all the small smiling things, the good things. He ceased digging and looked up towards the circle of trees southward on the horizon and saw Billy run towards him, something wild swinging in his fists. A dead thing or a found thing, Trey wished he could remember. Wished he could share in his brother's joy of discovery all over again, knock-about boys having a laugh, a mess around for the sake of mischief.

He wanted to add colour to the black-and-white memory but the inner demon was forcing itself on to him, like always when happy was about to settle, the devil-dog came racing.

He lifted the axe and swung it almost out of control.

'Hey!' shouted Lamby.

Trey shrugged and said sorry.

'You got an axe to grind with someone, I reckon.'

'No I int.'

'Should pace yourself. You go at it like a mental and you won't live to see the end of the day. Hey, you know what the only job you start at the top is?'

'No.'

'You wanna guess?'

'No.'

'Diggin a hole, hole diggin. The only job you start at the top.'

'Lamby?' said Trey and he threw down the pickaxe and picked up the spade.

'What?'

'Shut up.'

Lamby smiled and the kid-glint in his eye made Trey smile too despite himself.

'What you smilin bout?' asked Lamby.

'Nothin.'

'I know in any case.'

'No you don't.'

'Do double do.'

'No you don't.'

'You're in fancy mood.'

When Trey ignored him he nodded towards Kay working in the far distance. 'I knew it, knew as soon as I seen you seen her. Bang. I tell you it won't amount to nothin.'

'Shut up. Just like bein outside and workin and all.'

'This time of year,' Lamby agreed. 'But give it a couple months and not so much.'

'You still gotta work it through the snow?'

'What?'

'The land.'

'Course. Snow, ice, blizzards. Most volunteer for kitchen but there's only a couple places. If kitchen's full then they opt for slaughter. Int so cold in slaughter.'

'What bout butcherin?'

'Int much of that, most meat goes out in quarters, without its insides of course.'

'Don't the masters mind most work in slaughter?'

'No way, if they could they'd have us all there one way or the other. I'm surprised they don't steal the animals off the moor if they run out. Who's gonna argue with the lord?'

Trey wondered about this, wondered about the men with their sly eyes that said one thing and mouths that said another.

'Where they sell the meat?' he asked.

'All over, I spose, but most go down to the docks for shippin. Preacher's got connections on that score apparently. I always try get into kitchen in winter, it's the warmest place we got, all the ovens on and the pot bubblin with whatever.'

Trey felt a gurgle turn over in his stomach and he asked what time he thought it was.

'No idea.'

'I'm hungry.'

'You're always hungry.'

Lamby took a moment to stretch and Trey noticed a cluster of black-blue bruises circling his wrists.

'What's that?' he asked.

'Nothin.'

'Yes it is. That Wilder do that?'

'No.'

'Why he keep at you? What you got over him?'

'Nothin. Why you lookin anyway?'

'You makin a big show might have somethin to do with it.'

'Well it's nothin so leave off.'

Trey shrugged. It was nothing to do with him.

'Besides,' said Lamby suddenly, 'I won't be here much longer in any case.' He rubbed at his wrists and shrugged.

'How's that?' asked Trey.

'Got plans.'

'What kind of plans?'

'Dunno yet, but I think I know somethin and I defo seen somethin so, not long now.'

'You're gonna get yourself into trouble.'

'I won't. I got smarts just about.'

Trey laughed and said he supposed they all had plans but as soon as he said the words he regretted it.

'Tell me yours and I might just well tell you mine.'

'Not a chance.'

'You can trust me and really you can.'

Trey looked at Lamby and shook his head.

Innocence and high-jinks craziness rattled through the boy, an entertainment of a kind. There was also a softness to him that put Trey at ease.

Out in the fields Trey seized the opportunity to take in his surroundings. Up close the fence was a lot higher than he'd first thought and the yellow warning signs wired to it told him that he would have to scrap it from his initial escape plan.

'What's logistics?' he asked Lamby. He already knew the answer from talking to Kay but needed to pick the thread for conversation.

'Trucks.'

'Is that it?'

'Basically. The crates of meat go in the trucks and then the trucks get taken out of camp.'

'Who drives em?'

'We do, and then we leave em outside the gates for drivers to pick up.'

'How many trucks we got?'

'Just one, but a load of trailers, we just line em up outside and then every now and then trucks drive up and hook up the trailers and off they go.'

'How you get on logistics?' asked Trey.

'Thought you liked farm?'

'Just askin.'

'How old are you?'

'Fifteen, nearly sixteen.'

'You have to be eighteen. Only eighteen-year-olds are allowed to do logistics, it's drivin experience before they get out. Unless they're destined for prison of course.'

They went back to slamming and digging the ground and the thought of escape was so consuming Trey took a moment to push it from his conscience and he was happy to replace it with a little peace-wind blowing.

When the lunchtime siren rang out and he was near to falling he and Lamby went to the dining tent and Trey wondered where Kay had got to and he wondered out loud.

'Sometimes she eats in the stables.'

'And the twins?'

'Maybe the same.'

'What they eat?'

'Food probably.'

They stood amongst the usual complaints and were served and took their food outside and they sat beneath a tree with the plastic plates balanced on their laps and Trey mixed his plateful in together and stuffed the mash and beans until his chest hurt with the pushing stodge.

'Why int we gettin better food?' he asked. 'It's a basic for most, init?'

'Cutbacks and all, it's the govo's fault.'

'I bet they'd paint it up as good for the soul or whatever.'

'Them always lyin in any case. Three months I've been here and nothin that's bin promised has come to anythin.'

'Like what?'

'More learnin, like school lessons and that and sports equipment, not that I care bout that one.'

They watched people come and go and when Wilder and Anders and their crew stomped past Trey noticed Lamby sit up to catch his eye.

'You shouldn't do that,' said Trey. 'Makes em worse.'

'Who?'

'Bullies.'

'What am I doin?'

'Actin like you int scared, like you want a fight or somethin.'

'I int. Anyway they're gone now.'

'Still it int good.'

'It's better to stand up for yourself than not. Don't know why you're such a coward.'

'I got reasons the same,' said Trey.

He thought about what it was to keep quiet for the sake of planning and scheming and he had to admit that cowardice concealed itself well within him; he was just like everybody else.

'Anyway, I int scared of nobody,' he said finally.

'Is that so?' Lamby got up to take his plate back to the tent and Trey followed.

The afternoon pushed on with the sun slap bang sitting in the centre of the day and it slouched heavy across Trey's back.

He balanced the pick crossways on one shoulder and held it loose to let the blisters on his hands open and breath like tiny mouths and he wondered when hard work would become just work. It was difficult to think things over when he couldn't even breathe for the hot cinder dust that shrank his lungs down to rattling beans.

He pretended to survey the dry brick earth for new angles but knew it was all the same and he kicked at it to return the defiance.

'You restin?' grinned Lamby beside him. 'You takin a rest?'

'Course not.'

'Strong lad like you. It's funny. Not used to hard graft, is you?'

'Course I am.'

Trey smacked the pick into the ground and it made a not-much mark. He tried not to notice that Lamby already had some give coming into the earth and this made him swear into the wind.

'Just sayin, bit slow, int you? Nothin meant.'

'Well you meant that.'

'No I dint, just sayin.'

'Meanin and sayin's the same, if you dint know.'

They continued with the digging and clubbing in silence and Trey put his back to it to prove something to everyone but mostly to himself. He never was much good at anything but he knew mastery came with practice.

The relentless heat nipped at his neck and shoulders but he ignored it and he ignored Lamby when he told him to take a break. If this was the job he had to do then he would do it, pretend to those in charge that he was turning a new page over and over again.

He put some anger into it and he wondered what way the others would swing if they knew what he was capable of, really knew the core that was halfway to rotten with the demon and revenge thing rattling inside. It was there now; it was always there. It bothered him that they might find out and that thought bothered him the same.

'You like workin?' shouted Lamby.

'Course. Don't you?'

'I can take it or leave it. I like the chattin and the fun stuff.'

'What's fun bout workin?'

'The chattin, the camaraderie.'

'What's that?'

'This, mates chattin for the sake.'

Trey looked across at the boy to see if he was joking about the mate thing. The word had never been used with the bearing pointed towards him. It didn't feel right and there was no box in his head right for putting it. But still he kept it with him like an unknown entity that he might learn to like.

'Twins are funny, int they?' said Lamby and he came to stand next to Trey. 'Cus they both look the same and that.'

'That's cus they're twins.' Trey sat down and Lamby copied him.

'And they talk the same, dress the same.'

'We all dress the same. Maybe we should have numbers assigned instead of names.'

'I'd be number six, lucky number six. What would yours be?'

Trey ignored him and he turned his cap frontways to keep the sun from off his face.

'You got a lucky number?'

'Nope.' He watched Kay work in the distance and it annoyed him that she was at ease in the fields and just a girl and here he was a stocky lad with weak knees and soft hands.

'Two brothers just the same,' continued Lamby. 'I can't imagine another Lamby in the world. Spose that's a bullet dodged for everyone.'

'What's their story?' asked Trey. 'Why don't they speak?'

'Don't know exactly. Camp rumour is they was abused as little uns but I wouldn't ask straight.'

'Bin here long?'

'Three months same as me. Shy lads, they was, you wouldn't believe how shy, but I got em round with the old Lamby charm.'

Trey looked at him and shook his head.

'Don't know what they done to end up in here, spose somethin together. Them only fourteen. You wouldn't think so considerin their size, anyway, maybe they was gonna get split so they set some plan in motion, who knows?'

'I couldn't imagine em doin nothin bad.'

'Me neither. Them lads are as good as gold, kind of innocent, int they?'

Trey thought about Billy and his mood changed suddenly.

'You got brothers, sisters?' Lamby asked.

'Why you want to know?'

'Just askin.'

Trey stood up. 'Let's keep workin.'

'What's the rush? We're allowed a break.'

Trey went back to the digging with newfound determination.

He would smack and spade the earth until the end of the day and the days that followed and he would use the time to chisel away at his plan to find the killer and plot a way back to Billy.

CHAPTER FIVE

After several days of get up and go routine Trey was ready to greet the morning with optimism and he surprised himself when he took pleasure in the practice of prayer. He knew what was expected of him and with head down obedience he went through the everyday like it had been his for forever and when the work siren boomed out he was ready for it.

Trey stood outside the timber-framed stable with Lamby and the smiling twins by his side and he fought with the sun for idling shade while they waited for Kay to arrive.

'Gonna be another scorcher,' said Lamby.

'You reckon?' Trey reached out a hand so he could feel the heat on his skin.

'Funny how when it rains you wish for sun and when it's sunny you int so bothered.' He looked at Trey and smiled.

'What?'

'Happy anniversary.'

'What you talkin bout?'

'Bin a week, init?'

'Since?'

'Since you came to camp.'

Trey shrugged and said it felt a lot longer and he sighed with the weight of guilt that came from indolence and when Kay arrived in the truck he told him to shut up.

'Can you lads do anythin besides chattin?' she shouted and when she kicked open the door Trey could tell she had already started work someplace other because she was covered in mud and he liked that.

The five misfit farmhands took the truck a little further out on to the sun-baked moor and for the first time in that week Trey gained some understanding as to how big the compound really was. He sat bumped close to the yapping Lamby out on the flatbed as Kay crunched through the gears and he looked through the fence and out across the sand-sifted echoes of a once was seabed.

'Bone dry and burnt out,' he said to himself.

Lamby stopped what he was saying to listen. 'What?'

'The moor, dried to the bone, init? All that rain vaporised, gone.'

'Mostly like desert land this time of year, 'cept for the flash floods of course, and half the heather burnt just cus and we get the winters that are either ice-age or floods and then we all gotta pray for our lives all over again.'

Trey agreed and he added that things were never just as.

'What you mean?'

'The weather, it int never just middlin.'

'That's true and what's worse is we gotta sit out every little turn here on the moor.'

'And it's always warm,' said Trey. 'Even when it rains and then the storm breaks its always so damn warm.'

The two boys watched the landscape filter past in a rainbow of dirt-dust colours. There was nothing much out there that sculpted shape except moonscape.

'It's science,' Lamby said suddenly. 'It's chaos and it's science.'

Trey looked at the boy and shook his head and when he saw he was about to explain himself he told him not to bother and he continued to look at the moor in the hope that he might see flames.

When the truck slowed and Kay ran them alongside a ditch he asked Lamby who set the fires.

'What you mean?'

'The heather? Who burns it?'

'Farmers sometimes for managin, or might be a butt flick or kids messin bout. Smoke's somethin else though, worse than camp smoke. You wanna watch out for the smoke.'

Trey slid from the truck and he stood and looked around him for looking's sake and the world seemed slanted wrong with the sun way too close. Dad always said he had his mother's skin, he played out with Trey in summer to have him burn and build up resistance. He told him he'd have no choice if he was a fisherman with all that ocean glare, but it never worked.

He turned his cap backwards and sighed.

'Wish we had shelter today,' said Lamby. 'Just a stick-tree for dippin would do me.'

Kay shook her head. 'Gotta dig trenches all along this part of the fence, the whole edge of field.' She looked at Lamby and she looked at the twins and she told them not to bother asking why.

They toed the dry nothing ground and were slow to pull spades and picks from the truck and Trey wondered about the post-mounted cameras caught in the barb of the fence and he wondered about them all morning.

'Why's there cameras all round?' he asked Lamby suddenly.

'Why'd you think? Security obvio.'

Trey stood and rested his hands on the handle of the spade and he looked at the cameras and asked why some pointed outward.

Lamby stood next to him and sighed. 'Maybe they don't want people breakin in.'

'That don't make sense.'

'Breakin in to break someone out?'

Trey looked at him and then back at the fence. 'But it's electric, init?'

'What's your point?'

'Who's gonna bust a leccy fence?'

'I wouldn't like to think, maybe the immigrants, I'd say if they could bust out of distribution they'd have a good go at it.'

'Immigrants?' he asked.

'Immigrants,' said Lamby. 'You seen that long bunker behind the slaughterhouse?'

Trey shrugged. 'Maybe,' he said.

'That's where they live, and work, maybe even play if they allowed.'

'What distribution they do?'

'The meat of course. Meat goes farm, slaughterhouse, butchery and then distribution which is really the same as logistics.'

Trey narrowed his eyes to see if the boy was lying. 'Why int I seen em?' he asked.

'Cus they int allowed out.'

'That int right.'

'Course not, but they int legal so who gives a bugger?'

When one of the cameras angled down towards the two boys they continued to split and pick the desperate rock earth and Trey went at it hard with the shovel in hand and the anger that was in him was good for the dig. He thought about the red eye watching and turning and he thought about the impossibility of escaping this place and a little of his hope snagged up there in the slit-throat wire.

He stood a minute and looked beyond the fence towards the bundles of tinder gorse that begged to be burnt and he closed his eyes and inhaled the imaginary smoke and it was better than any cigarette. He held his breath to settle things a little and when he was sure he would not scream for fire or go kicking towards the tinder he opened his eyes. The camera was back on him and Trey looked straight down its barrel and he shot what anger the demon had firing inside towards the spying masters.

'You all right?' asked Kay and she stopped what she was doing and came to stand next to him.

Trey nodded, a nothing-something type nod. 'Why?' he asked.

'Dunno, you look a bit flushed. You want some water?' She offered him the bottle and he took it.

'How you likin farm detail?' she asked. 'One week on.'

'OK,' he said and he meant it.

'Takes a while to settle.'

Trey looked down at his battle hands and agreed.

'Takes time to get used to the fence and the armed guards and all.'

Trey shrugged. 'I int bothered with all that.' He knew she was looking at him and he drank down the water as something to do and when he passed the bottle back he apologised because he had supped it dry.

'I int great with authority.' Kay threw the bottle on to the flatbed and went to get another from the floor of the truck. 'Most in this place are the same but I really int great, I'm lucky to have the farm for doin what I want.'

'Time's your own,' said Trey. 'Kind of anyway.'

'Apart from the cameras.' Kay took some of the water and when Lamby started calling out the distraction was welcome.

'Is it breaktime?' he shouted.

'No,' they both shouted back in unison.

'Then why you breakin?' He landed the shovel he'd been using to flick the earth and came to stand with them.

'We're just takin a minute,' said Kay.

'Takin a break,' said Lamby and he helped himself to the water and jumped up on to the back of the pickup. 'John, David, you breakin?' he called after the boys and they shook their heads.

'I'm bored,' he said.

'Then get back to work.'

'I'm hungry.'

'Later,' said Kay and she moved away from where they were standing to watch a lone black SUV snake and rattle its way towards them.

'Nice car,' said Trey and he joined Lamby in sitting and idling at the back of the truck. 'McKenzie or DB?'

'That int no master,' laughed Lamby. 'That's the Preacher. The Preacher and all his guards and whatever else.'

'You sure?'

'Course. What you expectin?'

Trey didn't know but the sight of a holy man settled in a car meant for rich folk was not right and he said as much.

'Spose a horse and cart would be more fittin. Horse and cart and a barrel full of Bibles.'

Trey shook his head and he went to stand. 'That car int right for a Preacher,' he said again. 'Just int.'

He kept his eyes on the vehicle as it crawled cautiously along the uneven track and when the open passenger window came into view Trey glimpsed the man sitting there.

'The Preacher,' he said.

'That's right,' said Lamby. 'Spose he's come to check up on things.' Lamby passed the water to Trey. 'You all right? You look a little done in, pukey even.'

Trey licked the dry from his lips. 'I'm fine.' He took up the water and drank and all the while he kept his eyes on the SUV as it wormed through camp. If there was a moment for thinking this was it and he closed his eyes and he asked the demon who was blowing up a storm inside to be quiet to be quiet to be quiet.

'He all right?' asked Kay.

'Gone and got a bit peaky,' said Lamby.

'I'm fine.' Trey snapped open his eyes and he tried to smile but the panic that was in him came spilling and he knew Kay saw it. He pushed off the back of the truck and rubbed his head and he wished his brains weren't blown to ash in the heat.

'I'm goin for a walk,' he told them.

'You can't do that,' said Lamby.

'Watch me,' he said.

He cut a line through the fields where he saw the SUV melt into the hell horizon and when walking wasn't good enough he took to running with his feet digging spades into the baked earth. One more look was all he needed to see the Preacher's face. To see it was to know one way or the other, another step in his pursuit to find out the truth. In his heart he carried a sackful of sorrow and across his shoulders he saddled the burden of guilt. What it was to be alive when those he loved were not or almost not.

He told himself to calm some, couple thinking with the anger in order to take control.

With the breath pushed from him he stopped running and with each laboured step he thought out the best way to go at the thing that needed doing.

He went on towards the heart of the camp despite knowing that by going forth he was stamping out his own demise. When the demon told him to kill the Preacher he told it to be quiet until he knew things for sure.

Anyway this was prison camp. The Preacher hid behind armed bodyguards and Trey couldn't risk his own demise, the bullet to the brain same as Billy.

'Come back,' he shouted and his voice broke like a twig and turned to dust at the back of his throat. 'You gotta come back.'

He kept on walking towards the work buildings and then the bunkhouses and past the food tent and on towards the farmhouse at the entrance of the camp. All he could think was a hundred times maybe, but then again maybe not. It had only been brief in any case. A face in an open window, caught in an instant and framed like a portrait. If Trey could just see him a moment more he could scratch him off the list and go back to sifting through what he knew of the other men.

He crossed the clearing and when the SUV stopped Trey jumped into the shadow of the farmhouse and waited. He hoped to heaven that the Preacher would get out of the car and he waited for the door to open and held his breath in anticipation. He heard the door of the farmhouse swing open and McKenzie come into view and he watched him approach the vehicle.

'Speak up,' said Trey and he shuffled forward so he could hear the man speak. McKenzie was saying something about everything being good and fine and sorted and Trey could tell by his tone that whatever it was he referred to was far from it. When McKenzie stopped talking Trey held his breath and he closed his eyes to put himself back in that childhood cupboard. The Preacher spoke, once. Three words put out on to the air and they were all for Trey. 'I'll do it,' he said and Trey nodded, so would he.

When the vehicle skidded out through the gates, McKenzie returned to the house and the guards resumed sitting and idling in their seats. Trey emerged from the shadows. The Preacher's voice so matched in mind that there was nothing left to do but take out his lighter and flick the flame and it was like a great occasion he was marking. He held it to the stupid 'Welcome' sign and waited for the flare to take hold and then he ran until his legs gave out.

Trey stood at the top of the ridge where he had first found refuge and he watched the sign at the front of the house below come alive with the blaze and he waited until the rope burnt to dust and the detritus fell like a corpse to the ground.

He found the tree stump and sat with his hood in hiding and he took a moment to take in everything that he now knew as truth. He wished he could communicate with Billy this one time. Tell him that he had found their parents' killer, it wasn't that hard after all.

Down below he could see McKenzie jumping mad, the circling smoke perhaps a hint of things to come, a signal. He watched him kick gravel-dust at the fading sign and when the fire was nothing but charcoal remains Trey got to his feet.

As soon as he stood he wished he had waited a minute longer. If he had waited he would have seen the master return to the house and got away easily.

He sprinted down the rear of the hill despite its steep descent and he set a trail through the gorse-covered valley below to be sure of his getaway. It wasn't until he fell against a granite jut of rock that he stopped and he lay in the scrubland and looked up at the heavens in the hope that something might save him from McKenzie.

All that had been happy hope in finding the Preacher had ripped and was in danger of unravelling. Trey waited and he held his breath and he heard the man's voice and when his shouting became distant he got up.

Time dressed itself in the cloak of stupidity and it went slow and fast and indifferent and Trey kept walking despite the split above his eye and the pump of blinding blood.

He wiped the blood from his face and when the spill kept on coming he took off his T-shirt and pushed the cloth into the side of his head to sponge the wet. He kept on walking and the moor looked all the same. The one foot and then the other was all he could do because thought and reason had abandoned him, he'd set a fire and had nearly got caught. He kept one hand pressed to his head and the other worked his lighter over in his pocket but the usual calm he got from fire thought had deserted him.

He sat where he stood and everything inside and out was cinder burnt and the last of reckless heat circled him and buzzed his ears with surrounding sound. If he was to get revenge he would have to be smarter than he'd ever been. He couldn't risk being caught for something as stupid as small fire, get put in solitary and have DB and McKenzie's eyes on him more than ever.

He wiped his hands clean of sweat and blood and took the photo from his pocket and he looked at Mum and he looked at Dad and his thumb that had been rubbing face to face went to tickle Billy's into a smile and he closed his eyes but no matter how hard he tried the image of kin was slipping. Brother Billy was close to gone from life and near enough gone from Trey. He could not remember him and he hit his own head over and still he could not remember.

In this trance he heard his name rise and reel over the land and when the calling ceased to stop he stood up and he recognised the farm stables for the first time and Kay standing and she waved him over.

'Dint you hear me callin?' she asked.

Trey shook his head.

'Shit, what happened to you?'

'It's nothin.'

'Don't look like nothin. You should have that looked at.' She nodded towards the cut on his head. 'Reckon the swell's gonna take in some of your eye too.'

Trey didn't care and he said as much.

'Spose you can wash up in the stables.'

Trey nodded and he followed Kay and he kept his head down for the stupid that was in him and he waited for her to take the key from her pocket and unlock the door.

Trey thanked her and he was grateful that she didn't bother with the push and pry. He went to the bucket to sit and rinsed his T-shirt and bathed his head and for one brief moment the cool of water was a shroud in which to hide. He sat back with the bucket between his knees and let the water fall from his face like lace cloth and then he finally opened his eyes.

Inside the stables he could see the horses peeking from their doors and he watched Kay kiss what noses came to her and she told Trey their names but he wasn't listening.

He wished he was more settled towards level land like she was, had good grounding, despite knowing he was a distant shore from it. He wondered if it were a learnt thing or if she was born steady.

'You plannin on sittin there all evenin?' she asked.

'Nope.' Trey took one last splash of the cold water and got to his feet and he took the pitchfork Kay offered when she asked him to help.

With mindless duty Trey's mind stretched and detached from thinking and he half-helped muck out because his hands were red and swollen from the fall and his clutch as soft as valentine balloons.

'Where the others?' he asked.

'John and David are finishin up with the trenches and Lamby's gone to feed the cattle along the track some.'

'Spose they think I'm nuts runnin off like that.'

Kay stopped shovelling a moment and she looked at him and told him not to be stupid. 'You got too many emotions racin in you tis all.'

Trey shook his head but he knew she was right and he hated her insight and he loved it all the same. It was as if Kay had really seen him for who he was and not just in a glance but up-close looking.

'Emotions is a luxury you can't afford in here,' she continued. 'None of us can. You need to toughen up and if you int got it in you then you better start pretendin.'

'I wish I had the time,' he said suddenly, thinking about all he had to do. 'Int got no time for nothin but wonderin on things too much.' He looked at her in the hope that she might understand him fully and when she put down the shovel he thought maybe she did.

'One thing,' she said. 'One thing worth more'n anythin is there int no time for nothin but survival. You better dump that feelins talk, that talk int good.'

Trey nodded. 'But you won't say nothin, will you?' he asked. 'To the other lads.'

'Bout what?'

'Runnin off and goin crazy and all.'

Kay shrugged. 'Int no business of mine 'cept work might not get done. You better go on the run in the evenin next time.'

'I think maybe I will.'

'But take a torch, save you fallin worse'n before.' She went to the door and turned an ear to listening.

'You hear that?'

Trey stood beside her and he dipped his head out of the breeze that was running northward from off the distant ocean.

'What is it?' he asked.

'Shoutin, callin maybe.'

Trey listened hard. 'There's somethin goin on, some kind of shoutin I'd say.'

Kay locked up and they went down the track towards the resonating noise and they picked up speed and took to running when they saw others gathered up ahead circling the action.

A few cows were kicking and fussing out on the dirt track and Kay rounded them back into the field from which they'd escaped and secured the gate.

'What's goin on?' shouted Trey towards the crowd and he tried to push through.

He saw Kay climb the gate and he did the same and together they stood on the middle rung to look down into the ring of vulturous kids.

'You see anythin?' he asked.

'Tryin,' she said. 'Can't understand why the cattle were out.'

'Someone messin round?'

Kay shook her head. 'Somethin int right.'

Trey sat back on the gate and he looked at the cows in the field behind and then he looked at Kay.

'What?' she asked.

'Where you say the others were?'

'John and David are finishin the trenches and Lamby's feedin cattle. Oh shit.'

They jumped from the gate and this time Trey struggled through the unyielding crowd.

'It's Lamby,' he shouted. 'He's hurt.'

Trey knelt beside his friend with his T-shirt mopping and he asked if he was OK but anyone with a good eye in their head knew he wasn't and he told him it was going to be all right and shouted for help all in a muddle. He looked up when Kay joined him and together they pushed back the crowd and all the while they called out for help.

When help arrived it was in the form of DB and the nameless doctor and Trey and Kay watched as they carried Lamby to the flatbed of the pickup and drove off.

Trey stood and rubbed his foot into the damp red dust ground and his hand went to his lighter for comfort. 'Wilder, I knew well he had it in for him.'

'Wilder has it in for everyone.' Kay went on towards her bunkhouse when the siren sounded and she shouted for him to not go looking for trouble.

'Don't worry int my problem for gettin into.'

Trey picked up his blood-soaked vest and he went to the outside water pump used for watering the animals and rinsed himself and Lamby from the cloth. He strangled the red from red and put it on and the cold was welcome in the heat.

He followed the straggling crowd that had been ordered back to their bunkhouses and Trey looked out for Wilder but he was nowhere to be seen.

Inside Tavy house some boys were talking about Lamby but most weren't bothered either way and Trey wondered which was worse: hatred or indifference.

He sat on his bed until meal time chimed and he lagged behind the others as they loped towards the tent and he noticed the dark that was heading with encroaching cloud and was glad of the gloom. He looked for his friends and took what food was on offer without the usual bother and went through the motion of praying and sitting and eating alone with his head slung low from his shoulders.

There was something circling in the air that spun close to both delight and fear. A place that Trey did not understand and he wanted no part. When the noise became deafening he got up to leave but the two older boys who supervised the entrance told him everybody had to wait.

'Wait for what?' he asked.

'McKenzie.'

Trey returned to his seat and he thought about what it was McKenzie had to say and he hoped it was to do with Lamby. To send a warning shot towards the bully boys would have been something.

'Fire,' shouted a voice from the back of the tent. 'There's bin a fire.'

Trey turned to watch McKenzie part the crowd as he walked to the front of the tent and he told everybody to sit.

'Somebody has set fire to the camp sign.' He put his hand to his chain and looked over his audience for signs of guilt and when his eyes met Trey's he put his head down and his hand to his lighter.

'Burnt it clean to the ground,' he continued. 'Could've burnt the farmhouse down if I weren't there to put it out.'

Trey felt the demon twitch with pride and he swallowed it back into his gut. He wished he had the nerve to ask about Lamby, just stand up and shout it and have the master answer in front of everyone. Keeping up a front was the only thing that mattered to those running Camp Kernow, keeping the kids in line no matter how bowed and beat and bloody they stood.

He watched McKenzie wind himself up for the sake of show but Trey no longer listened and he looked at his hands for the pick and when he returned his gaze to the master he saw Wilder standing beside him.

When the boy saw Trey looking he waved for him to join them and Trey scraped at his empty plate, pretending he hadn't seen him. The boy was bad and he knew it and he wondered why he himself was anywhere close to his radar except as another boy to bully.

He kept his head down and when McKenzie left he saw an opportunity to get gone. He tipped his cap forward and ducked from the tent and headed back to the bunkhouse.

He pulled off his wet T-shirt and lay on his back and with the giddy that came from the knock to his head and he allowed the swim to guide him towards some kind of concussed sleep.

In that state of near drowning the young boy Trey played out on the headland close to home and his wishing and praying was all for Billy because the boy that was both protector and friend had gone. Not far and not away, but the boy that was big brother had been taken from Trey. He saw the chapel and the gravestones laid snaggle-tooth in the clay yard and everyone standing black and serious and stony, staring out to sea like statues waiting for the next storm to come crashing in.

Trey knew this dream and he knew it well and no matter how far he ran from it, to dare himself to turn was to see that steeple and the black and the black and the black. It was a place of dread and of terror but each night he knew he would go back. To return to the nightmare was to try in vain to pare partial guilt from his bones. It was a lonely place but Trey had got used to being alone.

CHAPTER SIX

Trey woke the following morning with fear balanced dead weight against his chest and he sat up and looked over at Lamby's bed. At the far end of the room he could see the door had not been locked because a little daylight flashed there occasionally when the wind blew and Trey guessed DB had forgotten to lock it because of yesterday's commotion.

He glanced around him and some boys were stirring and he saw Wilder, his wide mouth moving with unconscious ramblings.

He sloped from off the bed and silently he carried his trainers across the room and through the door. Outside he crouched to tie his shoes and he went to splash his face in the shower-block sink. He stood and contemplated his reflection in the one good mirror and poked at the split-lip and the purple circling his left eye, plum stained and darkening, and he sighed because there was nothing he could do to change it.

He splashed his face over and dried it on his sleeve and went outside to sit in the first shade and waited for the siren to call him to breakfast. His head still spun heavy with hurt and a billion thoughts jammed within.

Some kids came and sat in the yard but most went on towards the tent and when he saw Kay appear through the early heat haze he waved her over.

'Anyone bother bout your shiner yet?' she asked.

'Int seen anyone worth askin.'

'Wilder bother you?'

'Nope.'

'You bothered him?'

'Nope.'

She stood with the sun in a halo above her head and he squinted to look up at her and it was then he noticed the teal clouds on the horizon. Their formation meant a storm was coming.

'You heard anythin bout Lamby?' he asked.

'Course not.' She sat next to him on the ground and they both had wondering and worry squashed tight between them.

'Spose he's OK. We'd hear somethin otherwise.'

'I wouldn't bet on it. Int nothin honest in this place.' Kay stood and smacked the dirt from her jeans and said she was going to breakfast.

In the meal tent everything was just about normal.

They sat opposite to the twins and said their prayers and they ate and drank what was given.

'Tastes worse than ever,' said Trey.

Kay nodded. 'Maybe cus your mouth's mashed up.'

'Int that bad, I just looked.'

'Tis. Swole like a bee got you.'

Trey hung his head and kept his eyes buried in his bowl, shame was at him and it split him and exposed him fully.

He spooned what was left on his plate into his mouth and because he knew it was swollen he felt the sting and when he saw Wilder and Anders stomp a trail through the tent something in him bit between his teeth, an agitation that itched almost out of control.

McKenzie entered the tent and all eyes fell to the floor except Wilder and Trey wondered about his bullet balls and when the master looked at him he wondered about his own. He scraped at his bowl and listened to the closeness of sudden circling footsteps and he knew they were coming for him and he sat back and waited.

'What's this?' McKenzie asked, the chain snaking against his hip.

'Nothin, sir,' said Trey.

'Funny-lookin nothin, Rudeboy.' He held Trey's chin in one hand and turned him left and right. 'Spose you fell.'

'Yes, sir.' The touch of the man's hand against his face made him stiffen with fury.

'Spose you fell in a tumble.'

Trey nodded.

'You on farmin, Rudeboy?'

'Yes, sir.'

'Like it, do you?'

'It's OK, all right, I spose.' There was no point in lying. McKenzie reckoned he had been fighting. He was going to get it either way.

'Shame you had an accident, init?'

'Yes, sir.'

'Farm life int for Rudeboy after all.' He brushed Trey's hair from his face and Trey's skin crawled cold with creepies.

'Shame,' the man smiled and snapped back his hand. 'Spose I got space in the chop-shop butchery, a little corner to work for a clumsy clot like you. Can I trust you with a blade?'

Trey nodded. 'Yes, sir.' He tried to smile to keep the bother at bay but his skin had gone from creepy cold to peeling hives of heat.

'Good boy, get you down to butchery when the siren goes.'

Trey kept smiling and he felt his swollen lip split and drip red and from the corner of his eye he could see Wilder laughing and he wondered why he was not the one being punished for fighting.

'You're bleedin,' said Kay when he sat back to face her.

'Can't believe this, all I wanted was to keep my head down and my mouth shut.'

Trey wished Kay would say patch-up words to make him feel better but knew she wasn't that kind of girl and he looked at John and then David and they both shrugged sympathy and that was something. He got up and made his way to the butchery and he sat on the step below the hot tin building with the damp air of storm crawling close and he fantasised about the reality of having a knife in his hand. He got in line when he saw the others queue at the door and nobody spoke.

'What's your name?' asked an older boy standing at the entrance.

'Trey.' He looked down at the boy's supervisor badge, his name was Jack.

'You ever worked in a butcher's before?'

'Course not.'

Jack looked at him and marked him as trouble and Trey asked if he could go in.

'Best you stand a while and watch the others at work.'

Trey nodded and pushed past.

'Not too long though,' he shouted after him.

'No,' said Trey.

'No what?' The boy was behind him.

Trey shrugged and somebody whispered 'sir' in his ear.

'No, sir, course not, sir.' Trey shrugged and got elbowed for his troubles.

Inside the large, low-ceiling room Trey took a moment to cough the retch from his throat and he held his nose to pinch the smell of putrid flesh from his lungs.

'It stinks in here,' he said to Jack.

'You get used to it.'

'Don't think I will.'

'Course you will, it's just meat. Now sign your name for the knife.'

Trey did what he was told and he followed the boy to the line of woodblocks in the centre of the room to watch the other kids work the meat.

'When you're ready get on and do the same, it int hard.'

'How I know?'

The boy passed Trey the knife that was meant for paring flesh from bone and he told him it was in his interest to learn fast.

'Firstly slaughter do the kill and gut,' shouted the girl beside him, 'then we do a basic crack in half and then you break each half into parts.'

Trey passed the knife from hand to hand and he thumbed the blade for the ping.

'Watch,' she shouted and she slammed the cleaver she had in hand clean through the centre of the animal and she was a good ten minutes hammering the rounded blade into flesh and bone until the animal became two. 'Easy.' She smiled, panting.

Trey watched her claw her fingers into the cows ribs and wrench it apart and for the second time his hand went to his mouth.

'Slaughter don't always cut out all the bits and bobs,' the girl continued. 'So make sure to scrape and hollow before you start cuttin em and then someone will come and hook what you done away.'

Trey removed himself mentally from the nothing work and he put his back to the thing for the sake of obedience and several hours were lost that way despite the nausea rising, replacing anger.

The sight of blood was in every corner of looking, every kid with their fingers caked in gore and the smear of a once was life in their hair and on their skin. Trey wondered about their casual chatter and the ease of their hands and he wanted to shout for the wrongness of it all.

All the while his head pounded with pain from the fall and his fingers grappled and cut where the flesh allowed and it was as if the parts had lives of their own. He wondered where the meat might go and imagined the tables set pretty and the greedy gobbling mouths waiting to take life for the sake of life.

'Spose this is child labour,' he shouted to the girl. 'Kind of anyway.'

'Keeps us busy, don't it?' she puffed.

'I can think of better things to do.'

The girl stopped to catch her breath. 'I used to work logistics, bloody loved workin logistics.'

'What happened?'

'Got moved cus of my size. You can say it, I'm a big girl.'

'What's size got to do with it?'

'All that crate liftin and runnin round, I spose.'

'But you're strong, that int fair, you should get some say in it.'

The girl laughed. 'Don't let anyone know you enjoy whatever work it is you're enjoyin.'

'Don't plan on hangin round long enough to settle on enjoyin somethin.'

Trey wondered what trade it was they were supposed to be learning apart from abetting murder and he was about to say as much when he saw McKenzie enter the building. He watched him walk the aisle with his chain coiling in his hand and he slapped the benches where the workers had slowed and Trey was quick to keep his head down. The air was thick with surplus oxygen as everyone held their breath and they waited for the master to leave but instead he stood at the door and he shouted lunch and he shouted the name of the kid who would not be going to lunch. The slowest worker of the day would be spending it in isolation with him.

Trey breathed a sigh of relief and he returned the knife and followed the others out of the building and into the fiddling mizzle-rain and they headed towards the food tent. His feet hurt from standing longer than what he was used to and still he stood and he took the limp sandwich offered and a bottle of tepid tap water and he went back out into the drear to look for Kay and the twins. He missed them and he didn't mind admitting that he also missed Lamby; he hoped he was doing OK.

He stuffed the sandwich and took the quickest route that led to the farm and he went to the stables and then to the cows and stood on higher ground and cupped his hand over his eyes to keep the wet from blinding until he saw Kay at work in a distant field.

'Hey,' he shouted when he got close enough to be heard.

'You come to help?' She put down the pickaxe that swung from her arms and pushed it towards him with her foot.

'Nope.' He shrugged.

'So what's up?'

'Say hello, I dunno.' He shifted his feet in the muddy suck and waited for her to speak and when she didn't he said something about butchery being boring.

'I know,' she nodded. 'Same old over and over, init?'

'Just bout, I'm good at cuttin,' he lied. He watched Kay for signs of interest but instead she picked up the pickaxe and continued to churn the ground over and Trey stood dangling.

'You hear bout Lamby yet?' he asked.

'No.'

'Anythin?'

'If I did I'd say.'

'Wish the masters would tell us somethin.'

'Maybe there int nothin to tell.'

'Still they should say, maybe I should go ask the chaplain.'

Kay stopped what she was doing and Trey's eyes traced the arch of muscle as she cradled the heavy tool in her arms and he noticed the weave of scars across her back and shoulders.

She rolled the pick on to the ground and folded her arms. 'If there's things not right it int good to go meddlin.'

Trey folded his arms the same. 'I know that much.'

They stood like mirrors reflecting similarities and the spark of theories bounced between them until the siren went up and lunch was over and Kay turned back to her work.

Trey returned to the centre of camp and when the red-stained slaughter kids came into view he joined them in heading towards the butchery.

'Where did you go?' asked Jack.

Trey shrugged and asked why it mattered.

'Security is what matters.'

'I got me lunch, did what I was sposed.' He signed for the knife and looked at the boy and asked what else was wrong.

'You weren't told to go walkabout.'

'I went down farm.'

'You don't work down farm no more. You're sposed to stay with your work detail and you're drippin mud and water all over.'

Trey didn't know what to say so he said nothing and he went over to the butcher's block and when a carcass slammed his way he was ready for the slash and scoop.

He wiped his face dry and listened to the conversation between the girl beside him and another boy.

'It's happened before,' the girl shouted above the chopping. 'Few times, I reckon. Remember the time that crazy lad tried to escape? Climbed the fence when the leccy went bust and then they got it back working without checkin the perimeter.'

'What happened?' asked the boy.

'What you think? Poor bugger got fried, whole camp smelt of pork and you know we don't work pig. Anyway, camp went on mental shut-down after that, stricter than strict and now here we go again.'

'What you reckon's goin on?' asked Trey.

The girl put down her meat cleaver, she was enjoying the attention. 'The usual, I spose, someone done somethin they int sposed, that sort of thing.'

Trey thought about Lamby and he wondered about the secret he was forever alluding to.

'Where kids go if they need a doctor?' he asked suddenly. 'I mean emergency doctor, like hospital?'

'Military down west, rough hole with high security by all accounts, I should know, had me baby down there last year.'

'What happened?'

'What you mean?'

'The baby, what happened to it?'

'How should I know? Worse fourteenth birthday I ever had, no booze no fags nothin.'

When Jack came around with the 'shut-up' on his lips everyone went back to working the meat and Trey kept his thoughts to himself because of the confusion scattered there.

When the work day was done and they were told to go to the bunkhouses Trey was glad of it. His back ached with the lifting of meat and his hands throbbed with the intricacy of working a blade.

He stood outside the building and watched the others kick idle towards the shower block and he went some way with them until alone and he headed towards the farm to wait for Kay. He leant against the stable wall and watched the gathering storm clouds crash and clamber for attention and he knew it wouldn't be long before the rain returned proper to split the rocks and run rivers where the dry-snap tracks once lay.

He folded his arms in defiance and when Kay came striding over the hill he shouted for her to hurry because covert knowledge was a heavy weight to carry alone.

'Can't believe this,' she shouted. 'Bastards took my truck.'

She stood beside him and lit herself a cigarette and this time it wasn't for sharing.

'What you mean?' asked Trey.

'When they took Lamby to hospital they never returned it. How am I sposed to work without a truck, I mean really.'

Trey waited for her to smoke some for the calm and when a minute passed he told her what he'd heard in the way of rumour that somebody had said or done something they shouldn't have.

'You think Lamby's behind it?' She went to unlock the stable door.

They went into the gloom and Kay pulled up a bale of hay for sitting and Trey did the same and when she finished her cigarette he asked for the butt and she gave it to him for the final pull.

'The masters seem different,' said Trey.

'How?'

'Stricter. This is a strange kind of camp. Strangest, I reckon.'

Kay shrugged and said it was the only place she knew other than street living.

'You reckon somethin's goin on we int allowed to know?'

'Int that always the case?'

'Spose, but what if Lamby's in trouble?'

'You think he is?'

Trey shrugged and nodded in a mix and then he said 'yes' he thought he was.

'Maybe that's why he got beat. Int much we can do if he's in hospital,' she said.

'No ambulance came for him.'

'That's cus they took my damn truck.'

Trey took out his lighter to help him think and when he flicked the flint Kay told him to put it away. Through the dim he could see she was looking at him and he was glad of the muted light because he could feel the familiar burn of embarrassment rise up in his cheeks.

'So how's you?' she asked.

'Fine,' he lied and he shrugged and said something stupid about working.

'Bout yesterday.'

'Bout Lamby?'

'Bout you stupid.'

Trey glanced around the stables and he wondered if he could play down the thing that was too crazy to explain.

'Nothin,' he said at last. 'Just this place, takes some gettin used to.'

'Don't lie.'

'I int lyin.'

'Sounds like you is, thought you liked rules and regs and all that.'

Trey looked across at the girl with the honesty everywhere about her and he smiled because this was one person and the only person who bothered to listen.

'Stuff is all,' he said. 'Stuff inside gets me angry, so angry it escapes whether I want it to or not.'

He sat forward and there was a part of him that was close to speaking and spilling guts.

'We all got that,' said Kay. 'I used to have that but it don't do no good and does nothin but harm.' She looked at Trey and shrugged.

'I'm all right,' he said and when the demon laughed he said it again. He finished with the finger bite and chew and looked over at Kay and he realised she had got up and was standing with the horses and the similarities between them were apparent, the need for freedom when both had feral blood. He watched her silhouette pass by the stalls and heard her whisper into their ears and he wondered what secrets she told and wished there was more telling to her than asking. If there was something about a girl worth learning then it was this girl; the girl with the mystery circling and the anger taken and put right.

He got to his feet and went to the door when the meal siren blasted and they walked slow for thinking time despite the rain because there was no point hurrying in any case.

They stood in the line of dripping kids and waited for the food that was rice and beans and took what was obvious as rations to the benches and sat down for prayers.

'This int even warm,' said Trey when they were given the nod to eat, 'barely anyway.' He looked up for the usual placing of people and he noticed Wilder had engaged the chaplain in some kind of quiet dispute.

'Look,' he said to Kay and he nodded towards them. 'What you reckon?'

Kay looked up and then she settled back to eating. 'Them two don't get on.' She looked up at Trey. 'When I say don't get on, I mean Wilder don't like the chaplain.'

'Why not? He's about the only decent one in here.'

'On account of just that, Wilder don't do decent.'

Trey watched for clues to Lamby and watched for clues of the Preacher and there was something in Wilder that Trey realised had been there when he first met him; he was secretive and dangerous and Trey couldn't take his eyes off the boy nor his mind from the fact he knew more than most.

When he heard his name he turned to Kay and he realised she had been asking him a question.

'What?' he asked.

'You want puddin? I'm goin up.'

Trey nodded and he went back to looking until he saw Wilder storm from the tent.

'He int got no respect,' he said to himself and he remembered Billy had taught him everything right and wrong and all that lay between.

He watched the chaplain disappear from view and Kay come in his place and he took the apple that was meant for pudding and they both laughed and when the twins joined them they all laughed more.

'I got news,' she said when she settled to sitting.

'Bout Lamby?' Trey asked.

'Bout the Preacher, he might be on his way back.'

Trey bit hard into the apple and a bit of lip went in with the thrill of the moment.

'When?' he asked.

'Soon is all I know. It int good anyway. Preacher only means one thing and that's somethin int right.'

Trey wiped the blood from his lip. 'We know that, don't we?'

Kay shrugged and when they were told there would be no free time tonight and to head to their bunkhouses she turned to Trey and agreed.

Outside the tent Trey was quick to get to the bunk-house for peace and planning and when he saw the chaplain beckon towards him he looked down at his feet and when he heard him call out his name there was nothing more he could do because of the polite that was in him and he stopped and waited.

'Tremain,' the man shouted. 'Tremain Pearce, init?'

Trey nodded.

'Been meanin to catch you.'

'I int got nothin to do with Wilder,' said Trey. 'We int friends or nothin.'

'I wanted to give you somethin.'

The chaplain reached into his pocket and Trey stood stony and waited.

'This is yours, init?' He told Trey to open his hands.

'Dad's watch.' Trey started to smile. 'Dad's watch,' he said over.

'I noticed DB had it in his office and I read the inscription and, well, it just int right keepin somethin like that when it int meant.'

Trey wanted to thank him but there were no words in him that came close to how he felt and when the chaplain left he went to the bunkhouse and sat on his bed to finish the sallow apple with the blood stained to it. It felt good to have Dad's watch in his hand and he put it on. Something of Dad was in that watch and it gave him strength. It permeated his skin and charged through his veins like a drug. A remnant from home that was knock tough and through its resonating power Trey knew he would build back stronger than before.

CHAPTER SEVEN

Over the following days things in camp started to change. At first it was just small things that Trey noticed; the siren that boomed half an hour later in the mornings and half an hour too early at night. Each night Trey sat in bed with his watch firmly in place and he made a note of routine changes. It wasn't just that each night the masters locked them up an hour longer, there were other things too. Trey had noticed the truck had been spending more time around camp, making short trips to the furnace when usually it lay dormant for days.

The smoke about camp had changed too; it no longer smelt of the usual burning carcasses but other things and the smoke no longer bellowed black but white.

The next morning and the third since Lamby's departure and Trey stood at the butcher's block and he couldn't think of one single thing that was worse. He stood with the knife in hand and he waited for the first dead cow of the day to come his way.

He looked at the beautiful black animal laid out on the slab like a sacrifice before him and he told himself it was the business of morgue that they were working in. He stood back from the corpse. A few days on and he didn't want to be a part of whatever this was and he wished the body was the Preacher's. If it were, all this would be job done.

'I don't feel too good,' he said suddenly and he put down the knife and went to find Jack.

'I'm sick,' he told him.

'You bin sick?' the boy asked.

Trey shook his head. 'Gettin.'

'You gettin sick?'

Trey nodded.

'Well you don't get to leave till you get sick.' He looked at Trey and then he asked for the knife. 'Go get a drink of water. You got five minutes.'

Trey went to the bathroom and he went to the cubicle for alone time. He really didn't feel so good and he put his head in his hands to steady himself. He knew the demon was waking and rattling around inside and his head hurt from all the tower-block thinking. He had no more room for stacking thoughts.

Outside he could hear the rain running rivers across the iron roof and in the distance the howl of thunder and he could tell it was heading their way; a storm coming and closing in on the moor and the circle of camp hidden within.

He got to his feet and flushed for the sake of pretending and went to the tap for a drink and splash and that was when he decided he could take no more. Soon the five minutes would be up and in that time he needed to edge between the butchery and the neighbouring slaughterhouse and past the storage crates without being seen. He headed to the entrance hall and found his oilskin still wet on its peg and he wrapped it and hooked the hood and went out into the rain.

He went towards the farm and when he saw the stable door open he was grateful for it because the place was the nearest thing to a happy home.

He stood in the grey and waited for his eyes to adjust to the dim and he took off the wet coat and hung it on a nail in the wall. He knew it was early but he wondered if he might risk being caught AWOL if he went to find Kay so he sat down and waited.

He listened to the rain play havoc with its volume control and he turned his ear to the usual cattle call but guessed most were long gone piston dead and done. Through the stable eaves the wind pushed wet and warm like warning breath and Trey breathed minims along with it.

'Trey?'

He recognised the voice and he turned his ear fully.

'Who is that?' he asked.

'You know who it is, dumbo.'

Trey stood soldier quick. 'Lamby?' he shouted.

'Shush.' The boy climbed down from high up in the rafters. 'Shut up, will you, I'm a fugitive.'

Trey waited for him to reach solid ground and he asked him about his injuries.

'Just what you see, few cuts and bruises is all. I played it worse than it was.'

'Played what? Where you bin?'

'The injuries. I went to hospital, just kept screamin and they took me straight in the truck.'

'You're lucky Wilder dint give you more of a kickin.'

'Know that, don't I?'

'What you say to him?'

'That int important right now. You gonna listen cus you won't believe it? You might guess at it but you won't.'

'Try me,' said Trey.

They sat cross-legged to the stable floor and Trey told him to hurry up with the storytelling for once because strange things had been happening around camp in recent days and he asked if Lamby had something to do with it.

'Reckon so.'

'We was worried bout you.'

'Really?'

Trey shrugged.

'Really really?'

'Who beat you? Just Wilder, was it?'

Lamby nodded.

'Thought as much.'

'Well I kind of wound him up to do it if I'm honest with you.'

'Why would you do that?'

'Let me finish. I got Wilder to beat me, which weren't hard, cus I needed to get out of camp and let's face it the only way past that fence is beat or in a body bag. Anyway, off to hospital Lamby goes and before you ask why I'll tell you.' He sat up suddenly and smiled.

'So why?' asked Trey.

'To tell the authorities bout this place.'

'Don't everyone know? Does anyone care to know?'

'They dint know what I had to tell em.'

'Is this gonna take long? I got a headache.'

'Again? Anyway, I got to talkin with some guards who was Army Police and good-oh for us I think they took it serious enough to investigate, you know, with all the problems goin on out there, they don't need a place like this in business.'

'Lamby?'

'Yep?'

'What you talkin bout?'

'The drugs.'

'What drugs?'

'The drugs, the drug factory they got the immigrants workin at.'

'You serious?'

'Not normally but in this case yes, I seen it. All them underground storage bunkers, that's what they're there for. That's why we've bin diggin trenches.'

'Get on.'

'Trey, I seen it. Weren't meant to see it but I did. I was wonderin bout em illegals and how they're kept workin underground and the rest and so I went and had a look and then I saw it, rows and rows of plants, cannabis.'

'You seen it?'

'Promise.'

'How you manage it?'

'Broke in.'

'How?'

'Air vent, it was easy, just broke it open and climbed in and went on goin till I fell to the floor.'

'You int got no fear, have you?'

'Not much.'

'Anyone see you?'

'No cus I landed on a bunk and all em kids was at work. Least now we know what em do proper.'

'What you mean?'

'Growin cannabis, manufacturin and the rest, that's why they're here.'

Trey crossed his legs and put his hands in his pockets. 'What then? What they do with it once it's processed? How they get it from camp?'

'Well this is the best bit, I swear it is.'

'Meat,' they both said in unison.

'That sounds bout right,' said Trey. 'With all the work we're doin in butchers it makes sense.'

'How's that?'

'Got them animals chopped and stored in a load of crates. I bet there's plenty of room in there with em poor bastards. Where they take em?'

'Export same as we know they do. Down the docks in the truck but then it don't get shipped, ends up on the street.'

'The Preacher's got it all worked out,' said Trey and he stood suddenly because the fight was coming back to him.

'You reckon?' asked Lamby.

'Trust me,' said Trey. 'It's the Preacher.'

'You reckon defo?'

'I know.' He asked Lamby how he had managed to get back into camp without anyone seeing.

'Easy,' he smiled. 'I took off from hospital and headed down to the dock for the camp truck. After the unload I snuck aboard and here I am, stinkin but alive.'

Trey stopped suddenly and he wished he'd thought of this escape plan himself. 'Why?' he asked.

'Why what?'

'Why come back?'

'Cus of you guys, you and Kay and the twins.'

Trey stood a moment longer to look at the boy and it was as if he saw him for the first time and he was not just a friend but a true friend.

'You can't go runnin round,' he told him.

'I won't.'

'And even if you do only when it's dark. There's them out there that won't be pleased to see you.'

'Double won't.'

'And we gotta tell Kay.' He went to the door with Lamby beside him and the two boys idled until the lunchtime siren went up. They waited for Kay to appear and when finally she did Trey waved for her to hurry up.

'What?' she shouted as she climbed the gate. 'I'm busy.'

'I got a surprise for you.'

'What now?'

Trey stood back to let her pass through the door and when she saw Lamby standing there Trey couldn't help but smile.

'Ta-da,' shouted Lamby and then he put a finger to his own lips. The two friends punched each other's arms in play and the three of them sat circled to the ground and Trey listened as Lamby retold his story.

When he had finished Kay took a moment to contemplate and then she told them the immigrants had gone.

'Gone where?' asked Trey.

'Out of camp. I saw em from the top field, all jammed in a truck.'

'That's tellin,' said Lamby. 'I don't know what, but that's tellin, init?'

140

'We should go and take a look,' said Kay. 'I always wondered what the hell them kids was doin holed up like that.'

She looked at Lamby and before he could jump for some 'let's go' plan she told him to stay put and she and Trey would go to lunch and back to work and at sundown they would meet up in the valley with the gorse growing crazy so they could hide if they needed to.

'There's just one problem,' said Trey.

'What's that?' she asked.

'I skipped off work this mornin.'

'I don't know what's wrong with you lads. Why you always lookin for trouble?'

Trey didn't know what to say so he said nothing.

'You have to go back. Just make out you was sick and you went out for fresh air.'

'And then what?' he asked.

'How do I know? Make somethin up.'

Come sunset time roundabout Trey hid beneath a low-hanging hawthorn tree and he watched what little colour there was in the mizzle-mist sky take to the hills and disappear. The rain was nothing much now, but it had done a good job of filling the marshland that surrounded every rocky outcrop about the moor, turning it into plains of sucking sponge.

He looked at his watch for time and listened out for the others. When finally he saw them through the coming dark and there were four of them he was glad of it because the twins were big-bruiser fighting boys despite their good hearts.

They followed Lamby to the vent that was his first point of entry and each kid in turn dropped feet first into the building that would show Trey what he already knew: the Preacher was marrowbone bad. He stood next to Kay in the hope that he might absorb some of her valour and they waited for Lamby to find the switch on the torch so they could see. They went on, each one of them with worry and wonder in them because in a parallel life they were just kids messing and mooching for the sake of kicks.

'Follow me,' said Lamby.

'We are,' said Trey.

'It int far.'

They went from the dorm with the narrow beds boxed floor to ceiling and the glimpse of other lives worse than theirs had the demon up and punching inside of Trey.

'This int right,' he said. 'Bet them kids int even done bad and they bin treated worse'n dogs.' When they were out of the squalid quarters he gave a sigh of relief.

Lamby stopped and they all stopped and stood in line behind him.

'Ready?' he asked.

'Get on with it,' said Kay.

They waited while he fiddled with the bolt on the door and they stepped into the space and Trey felt the wall for the switch and he flicked the room into white-light being.

'It's gone,' said Lamby. 'There was plants floor to ceiling.' He looked at Kay and said he wasn't making it up.

'I believe you,' she said. 'Foil on the walls and em bright heat lights tell me they was growin somethin here.'

They went fully into the room and kicked at the filthy floor, each one alone in thought. Trey knew that the moving of the immigrant kids and the plants stripped and no signs left meant that they were more than ever in a world not of their understanding. The camp had gone from some upstanding model of correctional religious facility to a place of slavery and illegality in equal measure.

Trey hoped now more than ever that the Preacher was in reach. The camp was being closed down bit by bit and it wouldn't be long until they were split and packed and sent to other camps. The time was almost here to sniff the sly Preacher out of hiding, track him and kill him and get gone. Billy was waiting for him and he wished he could call out so loud that he would hear him holler.

'I'm goin back to the bunkhouse,' he said suddenly.

'But we int seen the other rooms,' said Lamby.

'We should go, the siren's gonna blow soon,' he said. 'I got thinkin of my own to do.' He said he would see them tomorrow and told Lamby to stay hidden in the

143

stables and there was something of the final farewell in his words. Trey knew it and the gearing demon inside certainly knew it. He looked at Kay and wished for a hundred ways to say what he knew he could not.

Trey left the room with the light pointing the way back to level ground. He unlocked the door and went quick through the storm to his bunkhouse. He sat out the night with the rain running inside and out and what was boy lay dormant and what was demon rocked to the rhythm and the rhythm was the beat of retribution's drum.

CHAPTER EIGHT

When morning came paranoia was a thing that crept about camp and with the new rising floods everywhere was quick in the swim of gossip. What was wasn't and what wasn't was and Trey had to keep his head out of the mire just enough to make sense of the situation as the siren demanded they head to the clearing after breakfast.

Trey stood in the yard in anticipation of news same as everyone else and he turned his ears from the talk so his eyes could take in everything.

The Preacher was coming and at the back of his throat Trey said it over until his nerves took hold and the universe and everything in it became something other, parallel. Trey knew once he crossed those tracks there would be no fissure or wormhole through which to climb and hide; the thing he knew he was about to do he would not return from.

He coughed and spat dry retch into the rising wet and watched it circle the other kids' boots and trouser cuffs and float from sight and he knew from the standstill silence about him that the Preacher had arrived. Trey looked up and he pushed forward to where a gap allowed him to see the face that he had etched in memory.

The Preacher was a tall man, cloaked and towering with big-boot feet that somehow gave the game away. He had elegance for a man his size, but Trey knew this was a learnt and practised thing, knew this man was all for the show.

'Take down your hood,' Trey said. 'He has to take down his hood.'

Through the cloche of fog and rain Trey tried to spy a feature of the man who killed his parents. He was certain it was him but to see the whole of him was to know for sure. Trey pushed into the crowd despite the flood water that filled the mud tracks and he stood below the stacking crates with the Preacher above and he realised everyone was praying.

The holy man stood with one hand hooked high above their heads and with the other he gripped on to the megaphone and maybe Trey caught his eye and maybe they held whatever it was between them in that middle ground that was both life and death. It was a place of limbo where they awaited their fate; the Preacher for what he had done and Trey for what he was soon to do.

He pulled the oilskin to his chin and gripped the hood into hiding and he stamped his ground as other kids crushed close and they stood like wet-whistle army recruits and listened in awe to the Preacher. Whatever the man believed it was almost believable, to the gullible and the soft-heads and the ones with nobody to show them the way, but not Trey. Perhaps to some the Preacher was a father figure. Trey hated that. He closed his eyes to get the focus thing set on the man's voice and he tried to make sense of what it was he said but it was brimful with God and Devil and Trey's demon took offence on both accounts.

'What he say?' he found himself asking.

'We gotta know right from wrong,' shouted the boy standing to his left. 'We gotta do what's right by the camp.'

Trey sieved through the words like grit on a shovel and it was as if he were gold possessed.

One nugget of truth was all that was needed to forge the metal that would finally seal the coffin. One nail bang bang. The coffin with the dead and the bad and the memories obsessed all in and bundled and buried underground.

'Give me somethin,' he said.

'What's that?' asked the boy.

'Why don't he give me somethin?'

'He's givin us a chance to fess up.'

'Bout what?' Trey moved closer because it was hard to hear through the drumming rain and the blurt of amplified voice.

'The kid who's bin spreadin rumours bout this place.'
Trey pulled open his hood a little. 'What kid?'

'Someone bin tellin shite bout camp. We're gonna be investigated.'

Trey jammed his hands into his pockets and he thought about Lamby and held his lighter tight.

'Do the right thing,' the man shouted and Trey nodded and he said to himself and anyone that was listening that he would. He would do the right thing.

When the Preacher was helped from the stage Trey was quick to follow him, keeping his distance as the man made his way through camp and towards the slaughter-house. He stood against a wall and out of sight behind a curtain of water falling from the roof and he watched him enter and waited and he knew he would be waiting a long time.

Two armed guards flanked the door and they stood with guns settled to trigger but Trey could see they weren't bothered about much except standing out of the wet. Trey knew inside any last evidence would soon be brushed gone and with it maybe his one and only and last chance to face the Preacher.

He looked down at his hands and noticed the demon had taken the lighter from out of his pocket and had struck the flint and Trey watched the fire and rainwater surround.

'We're goin in,' said the demon and he returned the fire to its hiding place and stepped forward and together they went to the men.

'I've left somethin inside,' said Trey. 'If I don't get it I'll die.'

'What?' asked one of them.

'Inhaler,' Trey lied.

The men looked him over and for once Trey was glad of his size. He looked harmless enough.

'Don't be long,' the second man said and in unison they moved apart to let him pass.

Inside the slaughterhouse Trey didn't know which way to turn. He walked slow to keep the wet slap of his trainers silent with the flavours of fight and flight coursing through him. Everything he had thought out in the way of murder had gone from him now. He tried to concentrate on the act of doing, but the memory of Mum and Dad tipped empty of life was too great, both of them nothing more than floored rag dolls, bloodless.

He slipped into the room meant for herding and gunning, where the last of the beasts hung bolt-blasted from the rafters on a hook. He slid the lock on the door and hid and waited behind the animal.

He heard talk approaching and then the Preacher came into the room and Trey was glad to see the phone in his hand because it meant he was alone.

Trey watched the man cross the room and when the demon told him to unclip the hook meant for meat from above his head he obliged and he coiled the metre chain around his fist and put the crook to his lips for the devil's kiss.

Everything in him and everything in that room slowed and Trey swallowed his breathing down to an irregular tick. He waited. The world paused in time and when the Preacher put his phone into his cloak pocket the universe stopped and waited for Trey to step forward.

'Preacher,' he whispered. 'Preacher, init?'

The man turned and smiled and Trey hadn't reckoned on that.

'You int sposed to be here, boy.'

Trey nodded and said that he knew this.

'So best you get on.'

Trey stepped from the shadows and he went towards the man in the cloak and in his mind they were equals.

'You don't remember me, do you?' Trey said.

'Why would I?'

Trey shook his head and he tested the weight of the hook in his fist. He could hear the Preacher telling him to get gone and the demon telling him to stay but all he could think about was that rusty crescent dusting up his hands. He looked up to see the Preacher's mouth chewing over and perhaps he was saying settling things and perhaps he was threatening and Trey gripped hold of the heavy chain and let the hook drop from his grip and he sent it once round for the crack.

He watched the Preacher slip to the ground like a melting thing and his ridiculous cloak spread left-right like broken wings. Trey stepped on to the cloth and the

Preacher who was just a man became a moth beneath his feet, an injured insignificant being.

'What you want?' The man shouted and when he tried to move Trey kicked against his back.

'What do I want?' he asked. He walked around the black and blood ink spill so he could see the Preacher without the hood and he said that he remembered him. 'I was just a kid so doubt you remember me,' he shrugged. 'Long time since but not so long as I don't remember you.'

'What?' shouted the Preacher. 'What you want, you little runt?' His hand went to the cut on his head.

'My dad,' said Trey. 'My mum and my dad and my brother is what I want.' He told him to sit up and he kept the hook swinging. 'You remember them murders eight years ago down by the coast? Sure you do.'

'The Pearce murders?' The Preacher pressed his cuff to the wound to stem the flow of blood.

'That's it.'

'What bout em?'

'Them was my folks is what bout em.'

The Preacher looked at the hook in Trey's hand. 'You wanna floor that hook so we can talk man to man?'

'No,' said Trey.

'I thought you'd bin adopted or somethin. Better'n what me and Dad could've provided.' He went to grab the hook and Trey pushed him back and the abruptness had him raise the weapon in anger.

'What the hell you talkin bout?' he shouted.

'Your dad, he weren't the man you think he was.'

'What you sayin? Why you dissin the dead?' Trey was becoming agitated and the demon screamed out for blood. 'Why you kill him?' Trey shouted and his voice broke with the rip of terror. 'Why you kill Mum and Dad, why you try kill Billy?'

'Lad, you've got it all wrong. I dint kill em.'

'I seen you, seen you stand over Mum and then run.'

The Preacher put his hands to his face and Trey thought it a strange thing to do and he could hear him whisper and he crouched to listen.

'I was too late,' he said over. 'Too late to tell em and too late to save em.' He looked at Trey and asked him what he was supposed to do.

'What you mean?'

'I went to warn em.'

'Bout what?'

'Your dad had been treadin on others' tracks a good while, movin into areas that were run by other gangs. Turf wars, it was.'

Trey stood up quick. 'What the hell you talkin bout?'

'Drugs.'

'My dad weren't into drugs.'

'No he weren't, but he trafficked em. Don't you remember his trawler? Headin out into the Channel to meet up with other boats and then headin back.'

'He was a fisherman,' shouted Trey.

'Barely, enough to cover his dealins just bout.' He sat up straight. 'You were too young to know the difference, Trey.'

The sound of his name from out the Preacher's mouth had Trey rub weak at the knees and he asked the man how he knew his name.

'Cus I'm your uncle.'

'Liar.'

'Well whatever you want.'

'I don't remember you.'

'That was probably best for everyone. Me and your dad never quite met eye to eye, bein in the same line of work and all that.'

'You're still in the same work,' said Trey. 'How you get to be a Preacher and deal in drugs the same?'

'Money,' he shrugged. 'Easy money pays for my church, the good work I'm doin and whatever else.'

'You int doin no good.'

The Preacher shrugged and Trey could see he was happy enough with himself either way.

'I int lettin you go,' he said.

'Course not. Why would you? I'm your uncle who tried to save your folks but I can see you got a need to blame someone so again I ask, why would you?'

Trey gripped the hook. He didn't like that kind of talk; it confused him and he knew it confused the demon because he had fallen silent.

'Spose you just want me to let you go,' he said.

The Preacher shrugged. 'That would be somethin.'

'And you wouldn't go after me or nothin?'

'You think I got time to run after kids? I gotta close down this place and go into hidin cus of you snoopin bastards.'

'That int no way to talk bout us.'

'Well sorry, kid, that's all I got.'

'Don't you care that I'm kin, if you're right and all?' Trey wanted to smash him dead, but what if he was telling the truth? Then it would be murder and murder straight, not revenge.

'I got kin closer'n you,' the Preacher nodded. 'Got a kid if you care to know, a little in-camp cousin for Trey.'

'Go on then, what's his name?'

'Joe,' he grinned. 'Joe Wilder.'

'Wilder?'

'Spose you know him. Nasty little shit, he is.'

Trey's heart skipped a beat and he felt tiny-sorry for the boy. Suddenly there were a million reasons for his behaviour and one motive why he wanted to connect to Trey.

'He know this?'

'Course.'

'Why you keep him a secret?'

'Cus I'm a Preacher, don't need no mistake gettin in the way, only let him stay in camp cus I had nowhere else to put him.'

'So why he called Wilder and not Pearce?'

154

'His mother's name, tis easier.'

Trey didn't know what to believe from anything the Preacher said, but if he was lying he could have made a better story of it.

He told him to stand up. He wanted to see something of Dad in the man's eyes and maybe there was something.

'You know what happened to them that killed Mum and Dad?' he asked.

'You don't need to worry bout him. He's already dead, overdose it was.'

Trey nodded. If this was truth it was good to hear. 'So why people say the killer was in camp?' he asked.

'What people?'

'I heard some police say backalong.'

The Preacher shook his head. 'Local cop, I spose, them always got a way of stirrin. Like they int got nothin better to do. You gotta let me go now kid, I've bin honest with you and you gotta let me go and you gotta let all this go the same.' The Preacher took the bloody hook from out of his hands and swung it across the slaughterhouse floor and when the guards hammered at the doors he told Trey to leave at the side entrance.

'Trey?' he shouted after him. 'Don't forget to save yourself in all this.'

'What you mean?'

'Save yourself, cus I got it on good authority that God int gonna do it.'

Trey turned and ran to the door and everything that he had known now wasn't but still a weight had been taken from off his shoulders.

Outside the building he stood in the rain and he felt it soothe the fire inside enough for standing's sake and when he thought he might keel over he slipped to the ground and sat in the soak with his arms hugging. The heat that was in him was cooling and it steamed from his gut and his blood and placed the vaporised demon before him. Hot air rising, disappearing, gone.

When the water became too high he got to his feet and all he knew and all he wanted to know was the anchor that was friendship. He went through the camp with the chaos that was struggling order in his head and made his way towards the stables. He knocked on the door and shouted for Lamby to unlock it.

The boy opened the door an inch.

'Just let me in, will you.' He pushed past and stood with a world of water and lies falling from him and he saw fire and four familiar faces circled to that fire and that was something and that was everything to a boy who had nothing.

CHAPTER NINE

Trey slept on into the first cut of morning and everything he had dreamt was of survival and it was all pitched somewhere between reality and blur. He thought about Dad and how he had talked to him in a sit-across dreamscape conversation sometime during the night. He had told him to do the right thing in regard to Billy and had called him a man and Trey liked that more than he could contemplate. It made him proud and it made him sad in equal measure. Billy was the one who did the looking out; it was never meant to be Trey.

He had been thinking about his family as usual and not with avengement in mind but with peace, just peace. He turned from the sweet-smelling hay bale and its heady heaven scent and watched as spaghetti strings of sunlight lassoed across the dust-bowl floor and he could hear the sniff and shuffle of horses in the stalls all around him. There were things he could remember and things he could not and he knew something of falling to the floor and something of the fall was in him still.

He eyed a solitary wolf spider spinning a web the size of a wheel hub above his head and a pinprick fly fizzle within and he wished he knew the secret to catching something without trying.

'What time you think it is?' whispered Lamby from somewhere close.

'Dunno, late I reckon.' Trey leant up on one elbow to look around.

'How you feelin?'

'Like crap. How long was I out of it?'

'Since yesto mornin.' Lamby came and sat cross-legged beside him.

'Where the others?' He lay back down.

'Dorms. You just bin sleepin, I thought it best to keep you here.'

'Did I miss much?'

'Masters have all gone.'

'Where?'

'Left the camp.'

'And the Preacher?'

'Gone too, far as we know. You hungry? I'm crazy hungry, we should go for a recce and get some food.'

'Sounds quiet out,' he said to himself.

'No sirens no more,' said Lamby. 'I can live with that.'

Trey sat up and put on his trainers and he went to look out of the top half of the stable door and he watched the rain ease a little to make room for breathing space. 'So them all gone?' he asked.

Lamby came and stood next to him. 'Chaplain's someplace apparently.'

They stood with their arms resting on the top of the door and curiosity got a pinch on both of them.

'Let's go look,' said Lamby. 'Get us some food, I'll bring a sack.'

Trey shrugged. Truth was he didn't care what they did; purpose had deserted him completely. He felt numb to the thought of future and numb to the past. Both truth and lies merged and tangled in him like thorns and all he once knew of Dad was leaving him now, a slow bleed purge to remove all memory.

He wished Lamby would go away so he could look at his photo for the pretend, salvage something from his childhood to make it part-way good. But instead he followed Lamby out into the wet and tried to direct his hopeless heart towards someplace other than numb.

'I'm starved,' said Lamby. 'Hope we can go ahead and grab what we want, you reckon we will?'

'Dunno, we'll have to be careful, mind nobody catches us fillin the sack.' He looked at his friend and told him again to pull up his hood.

'Why?'

'Keep a low profile.'

'You reckon?'

'I know it. Don't want nobody guessin it was you that split on camp.'

They saw signs of life in the form of Anders standing cocksure outside the food tent and Trey pushed his friend forward and asked where everyone was.

'Inside, you're late.'

'Late for what?'

'You'll see, where's the rest of you weirdos?'

Trey ignored him and ducked into the tent. The place was a scatter mix of hungry kids and the two boys kept to the perimeter to get a feel for things and Trey asked the girl from butchering what was going on and was told Wilder would not give out food.

'What's it got to do with him?'

'Int you heard? He's the big I am, thinks he's got the rulin of us.'

'How'd he get that idea?' asked Trey.

'Just decided, you know what he's like.'

'That bully,' shouted Lamby. 'We should do somethin.'

'I int gettin involved,' said Trey.

Kids were jeering and knocking into each other and the threat of fight was everywhere. Above their heads the air fizzed and bumped with question marks and when Wilder appeared the tent threatened to unpin itself from the earth with the interrogating heat.

'Fellow inmates,' he shouted and he climbed up on to the serving counter and stamped his feet on the metal slab. 'You better shut up cus if you don't you int gonna eat.' He cleared his throat for dramatic effect. 'You think you got problems?' he continued. 'Let me tell you, I'm the one with the problem.'

'You can say that again,' whispered Lamby.

'I've taken it upon myself to take charge of you sad lot.'

Somebody shouted for him to get on with it and Trey watched as one of Wilder's gang toppled the boy and dragged him outside.

'Likes the sound of his own voice that one,' said Lamby. 'Big stupid voice he got too.'

'Shut up, will you, I'm tryin to listen.' Trey moved closer.

'What's there to hear? I am great you are not, I am the boss you are my minions.'

'Where's the chaplain?' shouted one of the girls. 'Int he meant to be around?'

A few kids chimed agreement.

'He's around,' said Wilder.

'We wanna see him.'

Wilder sighed and Trey could see he was losing patience.

'Sly bastard,' said Lamby. 'We all know the chaplain's a pushover but he int likely to let Wilder put himself in charge.'

'Someone get the chaplain, will they?' shouted Wilder. 'If he's so bloody important to you.'

'He should be in charge,' shouted somebody at the back. 'Not you.'

Wilder ignored them but Trey could see the anger in him was rising; he was close to losing the one thing he needed in his life to survive: power.

The chaplain arrived and Wilder pulled him up on to the slab beside him.

'You're all right, int you?' Wilder asked. 'Int got no problem with me takin the initiative have you, old man?'

The chaplain looked down at the crowd and he put out his hands and waved them for the calm. 'I know you have questions,' he nodded. 'And some of you might feel a little confused right now, but I'm here to assure you that you've not bin forgotten.'

Wilder whispered something in his ear and when the chaplain shook his head Wilder pushed him to get down.

Trey wished he could say something about Wilder being the Preacher's son, but then he'd have to admit that some of that mad blood ran riot in his veins too.

'What bout the guards in the towers, where they gone?' shouted one of the boys. 'Why can't we do a runner?'

'And what about the authorities?' asked another.

Wilder looked worried, his brain working double time. 'The fences,' he shouted finally. 'The fences are still on and them stayin on till the authorities decide what to do with us. Gate's locked too so don't bother wonderin.'

'How's he know what the authorities is plannin?' asked Lamby.

'He don't,' said Trey and he looked at Lamby and said they should go for some food before things got worse.

They pushed through the mob and found Kay and the twins standing at the serving area and together they waited for the bit of bread and cheese and better-days apple that had been granted by Wilder.

'You got anythin else?' Lamby asked the boy serving. 'Anythin hot or drinks or diffo?'

'Nope. You want it or not? Just keep movin, will you.'

They took what was offered and when the boy turned to argue with the next kid in line they scooped up anything they could into the sack and ran.

'Miserly offerins,' shouted Lamby as they hurried through the tent. 'And not just that, a ploughman's lunch style miserly offerins.'

'Least it's somethin,' said Kay when they stopped to catch their breath away from the crowd.

'I was hopin for some of the leader's rations,' said Lamby. 'Least I managed to nick some tea.'

Trey knew it wouldn't be long before chaos took up permanent residence in the camp and as they walked around the compound he thought out everything they might need but when they got to the yard he realised it was too late.

Some girls stood arguing in the doorway of their bunkhouse with handfuls of clothes gripped between them and around the back they saw a group of boys outside the medical room preparing to break in.

'Somethin's boilin,' said Kay as they crossed the yard. 'Won't be long till things explode.'

'We should get more food and store it,' said Lamby. 'Stockpile.'

'Could do with collectin up wood and tools and whatever else useful,' Kay added. 'Might only be for a few hours till authorities get here but with Wilder in charge I dunno.'

'Sanctions,' said Lamby. 'Enforced sanctions, who reckons?'

Nobody answered him because nobody knew what he was talking about. What they did know was Wilder held all the cards, food and shelter and protection and more. All things counted and considered, they equalled power and power was the greatest commodity a boy could have. They stood for a while to see if heat spores would rise or fall amongst their campmates and Trey turned his lighter over in his pocket until its power seeped and settled skin deep. He could no longer think along sensible lines.

He stood and flicked the lighter just because and when he saw Wilder kick and shout his way across the yard Trey thought the demon that had recently left him had entered his cousin.

'Maybe I should talk to him after all,' he said. 'Maybe there's sense there yet.'

Lamby laughed and so did John and David, they doubted it.

'What you plannin on sayin?' asked Kay. 'Really.'

Trey shrugged. He didn't know what, but the boy that was blood and abandoned same as was still just a boy.

'Wilder,' he shouted and went to stand in his way.

'Not now, Rudeboy, can't you see I'm busy?'

'Busy gettin nowhere. What's the use?'

Wilder tried to push past him but Trey remained steady and he told him that they both knew this wasn't the answer.

'I'll get somewhere with em sooner or later, stand my ground is all.'

'Stand your ground on what? Bullyin?'

'Nobody's bullyin,' he laughed. 'Just gotta keep order is all.'

'Why?' asked Trey. 'Don't you wanna escape?' He looked at him for a long time and everything he needed to know was in Wilder's eyes. The boy didn't want to escape, he had everything he needed right there. It was power and status, but perhaps camp gave something else to the kid who was as good as orphan. It provided him with a kind of family no matter how disaffected.

Trey watched Wilder join his gang as they walked towards the farmhouse and shouted for him to answer but he was soon gone from the horizon.

They went back to the stables with wonder swinging between them and made a circle of the bales of straw for benches and one in the middle for the tumble of food and Kay said it was nicer than the usual breakfast stodge and she told them to save back the apple cores for the horses.

'You love em horses more'n people,' said Lamby. 'I reckon anyhow.'

Kay nodded. 'I like em well enough.'

'Don't talk back 'n stuff. That's probably why you like John and David.'

Everyone looked at the twins and they smiled as if Kay liking them was their ultimate goal in life.

Between mouthfuls of food Trey thought about what Wilder had said. 'He's a psycho, that boy, always knew it, and now all this gonna go to his head.'

'What we gonna do?' asked Kay. 'Toe the line or are we out on our own? We gotta decide what goes with what?'

'Food goes with one and hunger the other,' said Trey. 'I think we should play along a little, keep our heads down and an eye on what's what.'

'I int goin back to the bunkhouse,' said Lamby. 'No way José I'm sleepin in with Wilder no more.'

'Don't think we got much choice,' said Trey.

'What bout here?' asked Lamby. 'We were all right last night, weren't we, Trey? Let's move into the stables.' He looked at Kay and held his hands together in prayer.

'Maybe,' she said and she looked at Trey and shrugged. 'Maybe for a few nights, till we know what's what.'

Lamby jumped to his feet. 'I love this. Let's put it to a vote.' He smacked his hand into the air and the others reluctantly did the same.

'Yes,' he grinned. 'Democracy wins.'

'Won't last long,' said Kay and she collected up the apple cores and snapped them and fed a piece to each of the horses.

'We gonna make it like a house?' asked Lamby.

'Just leave it as it is,' said Kay.

'I'll put a few more bales round for sleepin.' Lamby grabbed the twins and together they arranged one of the stalls into sleeping quarters.

'How you doin?' asked Kay and she came to sit next to Trey.

'OK, I spose.' He shrugged and then he looked at her and smiled.

'You were out of it a good while.'

Trey sighed.

'Don't need to say why but if you do I'm here for listenin.'

'I want to say,' said Trey. 'But there's so much to process, I wish I knew how.'

'Bout camp?'

'Bout everythin.'

'Well just when you're ready.'

Trey nodded. 'Lamby got his pack of cards then.' He saw the three boys start a game of poker in the stall.

'He found them scattered on the bunkhouse floor.'

Lamby looked up and smiled. 'Almost a full pack.'

'Seems cards int so useless,' said Trey. 'Keeps him quiet anyway.'

'Takes my mind off food,' he shouted. 'Takes my mind off sockin that Wilder into the ground.'

'He found some old newspapers too,' said Kay as she knelt to light a fire. 'Just as well use em for the fire.'

Trey watched her crumple the sheets into paper balls and when a headline caught his eye he shouted for her to stop.

'What?' she asked.

'Let me see that a minute.'

Kay unwound the newspaper sheet and she laid it between them and smoothed it flat.

'"Mob Rule. Children as young as nine go on the rampage",' they read in unison.

'What's that?' asked Lamby and he and the twins came to sit beside them.

'Truro,' said Trey and he put the paper on to his lap. 'It's a local paper.'

'What's the date?' asked Kay.

Trey looked at the date on his watch. 'Last week,' he said and he read on. 'Apparently it's bin goin on all over the country, says society has broken down more'n before.'

'Don't reckon,' said Lamby. 'Can't be as bad as back-along. What em doin?'

'Lootin, arson, fightin, riotin in general.'

'What's the Army Police doin?' asked Kay. 'Int this why they bin on the streets for the past year?'

'And they're armed,' added Lamby. 'You'd think more would take notice of a gun.'

'Dint you see anythin while you were out of camp?' asked Trey.

Lamby shook his head. 'Don't reckon anyway.'

'Well that's us ruined.' Kay stood up and she put her hands on her hips. 'Int nobody gonna prioritise us now, is they.' She went to the store at the corner of the stable that kept broken tools and tack.

'What you doin?' shouted Lamby.

'Just lookin.'

'For what?' He got up off the floor and joined her.

'We've bin left to fend for ourselves.'

'We're gonna fight, int we?' Lamby grinned and Trey told him that to have no fear was to have no awareness of anything at all.

'We gotta be prepared.' She handed Lamby bits of farm tools that still had something nasty to them. 'Can't wait round for rescue no more.'

Trey agreed. 'What we got?' he asked.

'We got a scythe and a knife and a pitchfork with two prongs broke. What else? Two pickaxe handles, they'll come in handy.'

'A tool for all seasons,' said Lamby. 'I begsy that big knife thing.'

Kay gave it to him and she carried the rest of the haul over to the others.'

'Not bad,' said Trey. 'And we got hammers and stuff, what about the chainsaw?'

'No fuel. Don't much fancy goin at someone with that thing anyhow.' She sat and fingered the blade of the scythe and Trey could see her wondering and his wondering was the same. They were preparing for something that they didn't want to prepare for, something beyond youth and courage and reasoning.

'You know a lot bout tools,' he said to keep the things from becoming weapons.

'I guess,' she nodded.

'You bin taught good, whoever taught you.'

'What you mean?'

'Bout farmin and stuff.'

Kay shrugged.

'She reads lots of books,' shouted Lamby as he started to flip cards for a new game of poker. 'Don't she, boys?'

The twins nodded.

'One book, I read a lot of one book.' She passed the scythe she'd been petting to Trey. 'Just some old book from backalong, found it amongst the junk long time ago.'

Trey felt the full weight of the scythe settle in his hands and he stood up and stretched the ache from his bones. 'I feel like the grim bloody reaper,' he said. 'Feels good'n all.'

'Don't get carried away with it,' said Kay. 'We're protectin ourselves is all.'

'Who said we would?'

Kay ignored him and gave the twins a wooden handle each. 'For protection,' she said. 'Just till the authorities come.'

'Can I keep the knife?' asked Lamby.

'Long as you keep it down the back of your trackies. Don't need to be swingin that thing round till you need to.'

'When will that be?'

'How do I know? When someone comes at you with somethin bigger.'

'What you got, the pitchfork?'

'We'll keep it standin at the door, in case.'

Trey wanted to say how brave she was, how nothing fazed her. He also thought her too courageous, but there was so much more about her than he could think about in one given moment.

'We headin out?' he asked.

'You int.'

'What you mean?'

'You still don't look too good.'

Trey rested his wrists on the metal curve of the tool. 'I'm fine.'

'After last night you need to rest up and clear your head. You're the cleverest we got.'

'I guess.' He sat back down and the warm purr of flattery rested with him.

'Don't answer the door,' said Lamby. 'And if anyone does come knockin keep that scythe in your hands.'

Trey nodded.

'Brothers in arms,' shouted Lamby suddenly and he scooped the twins up from the floor.

'We're off.' He smiled and he threw the pack of cards on to the bale of hay beside Trey. 'Help yourself,' he nodded as they left the stable.

Trey flicker-booked the cards and he laid them out for a maybe game of solitaire, then gathered them up and pushed them back into the box.

He got up and said hello to the horses and he petted the bay that he was fond of because it was fond of Kay.

Through the thin-plank stable walls he could hear the occasional shout and he hoped his little gang would be safe enough and that they raided what they could because he was getting way beyond hungry. He drank some of the water they had stored in a dozen plastic bottles and felt the warm liquid curve and bury itself deep down into the hollow drum of his gut.

He leant against a wall and looked up into the trussed roof space and his jellied mind took him so far wandering he didn't know up from down.

He listened to the rain hammer out tunes on the roof and he found familiar chords in the melody and words that he had not remembered since childhood came to him in a song. He slid to the ground and closed his eyes and he could hear Mum's harmonies. When the song went round a hundred times and the rain turned back to just rain drumming he sat with his head between his knees until the need to cry subsided.

If Mum were really there she would make tea like back-along and Trey got up and set water to the tiny flame on the gas stove Kay had placed in the centre of the stables. When the water got to boiling he took up the box of stolen teabags and he made a pot and poured himself a cup for the sake of settling. He took his time to sip his drink and continued to hum the tune and he closed his eyes and for a minute he could have sworn Billy was there with him in the stable.

He could see him clear as day and he was a man that sat before him. Trey smiled and his brother smiled back.

'You're better,' said Trey and Billy shrugged.

'Spose you know all what's bin goin on.'

Billy nodded.

'You heard bout the Preacher and Dad and everythin?' Trey shook his head. 'Still can't believe it. Dad was a good man, weren't he, Billy?' He looked into his brother's eyes despite their fade.

'You knew, dint you?' He leant forward so he could be closer one second more. 'You was fifteen, Billy, why don't you tell me what you know?'

Trey watched his brother disappear completely and he knew everything in his head was made of his own imagining.

'I bet you knew somethin,' he said to himself and he opened his eyes to the revelation.

* * *

'Nobody gonna be escapin anytime soon,' shouted Lamby when he burst through the stable door and he made Trey jump. 'That fence is still on, you'd be fried soon as look at it, razor wire good as new all round. I don't fancy anyone's chances.'

Trey flicked the tail end of his tea towards him. 'I worked that out already.' He looked at Kay and asked if they had managed to get any food.

'We got some bits and bobs,' she said and she put a sack to the floor. 'Flour and oil and a bit of sugar.'

'We're gonna make pancakes,' said Lamby. 'The twins are gone to bag up some hens so we got eggs.'

Kay sat down and said she hoped nobody else had thought of it before them. 'Them chickens will be on skewers soon enough.'

Trey asked if she'd seen anything of Wilder and she hadn't. 'Rumour has it he's holed up in the farmhouse now. Spose that's where he'll stay.'

'We won't see much of him,' he said. 'He int so stupid to lead his men from the front.'

'Happy givin orders from the castle,' laughed Lamby. 'He'll be fine till the food runs out and he got no bribes left to dole out.'

They wondered what it would be like when the food ran out and they thought about the chickens and the eggs that might or might not be coming their way.

'At the end of the day,' said Lamby suddenly, 'you can't leave a bunch of kids alone out in the middle of nowhere, razor wire and electric fence surroundin em. You just can't do that.'

He boiled more water for tea and Kay said they should think about collecting firewood for when the gas in the camping stove ran out and the others nodded but their heads were still on the buzzing, ripping fence.

'Can't we switch it off?' asked Trey. 'Where's the electric comin from?'

'Underground,' said Kay. 'And don't ask me where from cus I don't know.'

'We could go diggin,' suggested Lamby. 'Dig till we find it and short it and cut a hole in the stupid thing.'

'Underground and outside the fence probably,' she continued.

'We could try to get into the underground storage, how far down does the fence go?' asked Trey.

'Far.'

'How far?'

'Really far, I was here two years ago when they dug it, trenches so deep you could be standin and still be buried alive.'

They all sighed and Lamby continued with the fresh pot.

'We'll have to get firewood soon,' Kay said again. 'Get it before we need it.'

Lamby stewed the tea longer than was necessary and poured it and said how he couldn't believe Wilder was living in the farmhouse. 'I mean in an actual house, with beds and everythin.'

When the twins arrived back everyone was happy to see them and they were happier still to see the chickens swinging in a sack. Kay put them in an unused stall and she threw in a bit of grain and straw to keep them busy.

'When will we get eggs?' asked Lamby.

'When you think?' she asked.

'When they're ready, stupid question I know. What's up with you?'

'You ask too many questions, stupid ones.'

'So, always have.'

Kay took up her mug of tea and went and sat against the open door and Trey told Lamby to leave her for a while.

'But I always ask loads of questions, that's just me.'

'Maybe you ask too many questions at once,' said Trey. 'Maybe that's it.'

'Just wonder this and that.'

'Well un-wonder it.'

'Just wonderin in case, like when will someone come for us and if they don't then what? Dint nobody listen to me on the outside?'

The 'what' hung in the air and stuck to the walls like cooling chip-pan fat and they all had it in their minds to worry too much about it.

'Spose your parents might be wonderin,' said Trey, 'if you int writ them for a while.'

'Bout that,' said Lamby and Trey could see some echo of guilt in his eyes.

'What?' he asked.

'The parents thing.'

'Go on.'

'I int rightly got any.'

Trey started to laugh.

'I int and I int lyin, not this time anyway.'

Trey looked at the boy and he looked at him a long time. 'So why lie?' he asked.

Lamby shrugged. 'Just always said it, spose it made me diffo from all else.'

'So you int got no folks and no home and nice bedroom and all that?'

'No.'

'You fosters same as?'

Lamby nodded and he smiled all the same.

'And I know you are,' Trey said to the twins and they nodded in unison.

'You know you're crazy, don't you?' he said to Lamby.

'It's what I bin tellin you the whole time.'

Each and every one of them was a looked-after kid. One year or two or more, and here they were, children in need looked after and protected in a wrong sort of way. Trey wasn't the only one with a million unfathomable worries strapped to his chest like a run of explosives.

He lit a small fire and they spent the afternoon playing cards like there was nothing left to do on earth and Kay sat at the door with the pitchfork ready and she didn't move or speak until a hen called her in from the intruding dark.

'We got eggs,' she said and she went to check and was right. 'Two eggs.'

She gave them to Lamby like a making-up gift and he took them to the fire for cooking.

'Why int you usin the stove?' she asked.

'It's a novelty,' he said. 'Cookin on a dot of flame is fun till it int.'

He worked with what pots he had and it was the only time he spent just plain doing.

When the time came around to eat they sat in separate worlds and fed on the thin-flip pancakes. After they had eaten they lay circled in the bedroom stall and sleep came close and teased and at times it came but mostly it did not.

Deep into the night Trey wrestled with his blanket and he stretched it and pulled it until his cheek was the furthest it could be from the sanding hay bale but still it was no good. He took the blanket and went from the communal stall and lay close to the nothing fire. He slept better when alone, safer.

He wrapped the blanket around and worked it top to toe and he noticed one small bead of light within the dead-eye coals and it reassured and absorbed him completely and pulled him towards sleep. He dreamt of horses running the open plains and he dreamt of Kay and they were all the same, wild and free with untameable spirit, and his thoughts plunged into the engulfing fire and it warmed him and if it wasn't for the memory of the burning barn and the screaming horses come alive in mind he could have come close to comfort. Part-dream, part-reality but everything feared and laced with terror. He could see their nodding heads, nostrils torn wide and teeth wet with guttural panic. His heart beat fast at the horror of it all, their screams were his screams.

'Trey, wake up.' Kay bent over him and she wagged the torchlight into his face.

He sat up and rubbed his eyes to look at her. 'You all right?' he asked.

'Course I am. What's up with the screamin and shoutin?'

Trey pulled the blanket over his lap. 'I int.'

He could see Kay shaking her head. 'You is.' She got up and turned off the torch.

'Bad dream,' he said to the dark.

'Long as you're OK.'

Trey nodded to himself. 'I'm fine, thanks.'

He watched her fade into the dark and took out his lighter for the comfort flip.

'Damn,' he said and he kicked at the cold fire with one bare foot. He wished he hadn't let the worm of weakness seep from his body. It was nothing, a nightmare, a memory mixed. It didn't matter. The coming battle was his and he was ready for it.

CHAPTER TEN

Trey woke with his body cocooned in a twist on the stable floor. He listened to the sound of the horses shuffling in their stalls and he sat up and waited for one of his friends to speak but he was the only one awake.

He lay back down and thought about his life with a clear head and Mum and Dad and the rubber-straps that until now had kept him bound, secure restraints that threatened to snap and sling parts of him in all directions. Somehow he had to escape and get back to Billy; he had to try everything he could think of to rid himself of camp. He sat up suddenly, there was one option left open to him, one option and the only option remaining; he had to speak to Wilder.

Trey was slow to put on his trainers and he unlocked the door and crept quietly from the stables and out into the damp mizzle morning.

He looked across the camp and the rise and fall of the wet pumice tors in the distance and the neatly pressed creases of the moor and he thought about what it would be like to stand on the other side with the shape of some kind of future paved ahead; a future without walls and fences and boundaries. He went on towards the farmhouse, past the bunkhouses with the doors sprung wide and the food tent drooping from the rain and stolen pegs.

He stood out on the clearing and shouted towards the house and when nobody came to the door there was enough nerve in him to step up on to the porch and knock.

'What?' shouted one of the older lads through the screen door.

'I wanna speak to Wilder,' Trey shouted back.

'What you got to trade?' asked the boy and he opened the door fully.

'I int got nothin to trade,' said Trey. 'Where's Wilder?'

'Restin, what you want?'

'I need to speak to him.'

'He don't wanna speak to you.'

'Wilder,' Trey shouted through the door.

'Watch it, will you.'

'Just five minutes.'

'He's busy.'

'Who is it?' Wilder appeared in the doorway and he stretched and pushed the boy back into the house in one move.

'Well if it int my mate Trey,' he smiled. 'What you want?'

'We need to talk,' said Trey.

'You come round to your senses?'

Trey stepped forward. He didn't know how to ask a boy like Wilder for something. It felt wrong but in the end he just came out with it.

'What?' asked Wilder.

'I want you to let me go,' he said again.

'Go where?'

'Out of camp.' Trey knew this would be difficult.

'Why you? Why you so special?'

Trey swallowed hard. 'Cus I'm you're cousin,' he said.

Wilder started to laugh. 'Killed you to say that, dint it.'

Trey looked away.

'What bout the authorities?' Wilder continued. 'You're a criminal, can't just let criminals out for the sake of it.'

'Come on, Wilder, I know you don't care bout any of that.'

'How you know? How you know I int doin what's right?'

Trey shrugged. 'Cus you're a selfish bastard.'

Wilder laughed. 'Such a shame, init, Rudeboy? Me and you got so much in common. It's a good thing you're givin up here.'

'Just let me out.'

'Why? Why you and nobody else?'

'My brother,' Trey said honestly.

'Boohoo on that score.'

'He needs me.'

'We all need somebody; don't mean we get it though, does it?'

Trey looked at Wilder and for a moment he felt sad for the bully boy. Maybe he wanted Trey to join his crusade because he was family.

'It doesn't have to be like this,' he said.

'Don't it?' Wilder shrugged and Trey thought perhaps he had got through to him after all.

'Time to go now, Rudeboy. Back to your little tribe of circus freaks.' He shouted this so his gang could hear and Trey saw the boy standing behind Wilder laugh.

'You all livin in there now, is you?'

'What's it to you?'

'Where's the chaplain?'

'Don't worry bout him,' Wilder laughed. 'That old boy is fine o' fine.'

'I int seen him about camp in a while, have you?' asked Trey.

Wilder ignored him and asked if there was anything else he could do for them because he was busy.

'Don't worry, I'm goin.' Trey turned a circle in the mud and he kept his mouth shut for all the roar reeling within.

'I'll be seein you,' shouted Wilder, 'and tell Kay to hold on to em horses. I heard em right nice to roast.'

Trey went through camp the way he had come and when he saw a few kids standing around the tent he told them that if it was food they were waiting for they would be waiting a long time. He went on towards the ridge with the scraggy trees and the stump where he liked to sit and he stood and watched the patterns in the sky darken and become one. When the rain began to fall Trey took shelter beneath the faint canopy of trees and he hunkered out of the wind and rested his head against a trunk. He waited. For one final thought to come to his mind and change from a maybe idea to a definite plan, he waited and it was a long time.

He thought about Billy window-sitting, staring out from a world where he did not belong. Perhaps he remembered that day Trey had visited so briefly; two brothers looking, leaving, gone.

Trey closed his eyes and he pressed his palms into them to stop whatever it was that threatened. Since the demon's departure he'd been left with a huge cavernous pit inside, a gaping wound where once he'd filled with anger and spite, but now all that was left was a hole, an empty bucket soul.

He'd come so far, so much had happened and still he remained in camp. Trey was never meant to belong, he never wanted more than what was owed him, revenge.

When the wind grew stronger he got up and he left the trees and stood on the stump and he shouted for the world to hear that Trey Pearce was not done yet. Wilder would not let him out, but Trey would find a way.

He jumped from the stump and went down the hill and he went on towards the farm.

'He's a mean you-know-what,' said Lamby when Trey returned to the stables and relayed the conversation he had with Wilder. 'What he said bout the horses, no need to bring the horses into it.'

'Just knows what buttons to push,' said Kay. 'Ignore him is best.'

Trey took off his trainers and put them by the fire to dry and he settled in amongst his friends and took pleasure in the comfort that he found there.

'Spose we know who's had away with the calves,' said Trey and he sat to watch the twins squat close to the fire as they took turns to stir some kind of stew in a pot not meant for cooking.

They sat fixed in contemplation and waited for their mug to be dipped and passed and Trey tried to make some sense of what he was eating but he got nothing but potato and the grain meant for animal feed. To have something in his stomach was better than none and he thanked the boys for their bother.

When eating was done they settled back to speculate in regards to the chaplain and Trey had a feeling there was something not quite right and he said as much.

'He int around,' said Lamby. 'If he int in the farm-house he int around no more, he's off with the rest.'

'But he wouldn't just leave us,' said Trey. 'He int the type to just go.'

'So who's in charge?' asked Kay. 'Not Wilder.'

'No but he thinks he is,' said Trey. He knew without a doubt they had been abandoned but the thought of the chaplain someplace in camp still bugged him. Perhaps he was his ticket out of there, if he could just find him.

'We should go find the chaplain,' he said.

'What?' asked Lamby.

'Cus it don't feel right. He int like the Preacher and McKenzie.'

He looked at Lamby and then he looked at Kay and shrugged.

'Why?' asked Kay. 'He's long gone.'

'What if he int? What if he's someplace left to fend?'

'They left us the same. Only reason some folks might bother bout us is if we escape and go crazy on the outside.'

'More'n likely they'll leave us here,' said Lamby. 'Leave us to fend or whatever, seems like no authorities is comin in any case, spose they couldn't care less.'

'Well I'm goin lookin,' said Trey. 'Chaplain int such a bad old boy and I wanna know if he's all right just to know it.' He looked at Kay to see if she agreed and she did.

'But,' she said, 'we wait till dusk.'

'Can we all go?' asked Lamby and he looked at the twins with his thumbs up.

'No,' said Trey. 'Just me and Kay.'

When the grey of storm-sky smudged into charcoal black Trey got up and put on his oilskin and went to stand at the door and he waited for Kay to do the same.

'Sure you wanna come?' he asked.

'Course. Why wouldn't I?'

Trey nodded. 'Thank you.'

The two teenage warriors left the stables in the pitch black fright of night. The sky was clogged thick with heavy heaving clouds and Trey could smell the metal tang of electricity in the air.

'It's gonna thunder,' he said and he kept his eye on the heavens until light sprang zip-wire crazy across the horizon.

'We bein punished you think?' he shouted. 'Punished by God over and over again?' He looked across at Kay and she shook her head.

'Penance tails up within. You only got yourself to answer to when you slap yourself over the head with it.'

Trey laughed, she had a way of saying things that were simple and complicated and perfect all in the same breath.

'You think we're born bad? Some of us anyway?'

'Course not.'

'But what if bad things happen right from the get go, what then?' He could feel the small child within jostling to speak. The boy that lived inside him before the demon moved in.

Kay stopped suddenly and she asked him what he was going on about.

'Bad things happen to the bad, don't they?'

'No, Trey, bad things happen cus they happen. It's just the way things are.'

'How you know?'

'It's called the chaos theory, ask Lamby, he'll tell you all bout it.' She circled in the mud and continued to walk.

'Science,' he laughed.

'Science,' she shouted. 'Now come on and watch where you put your feet.'

'I am.'

'Well watch harder.'

'It's hard to watch anythin when you got the torch and the rain's in my eyes.'

Trey heard Kay laugh a little as they dug on towards the upward slope that led to the farmhouse.

'It's like walkin in marshland.' Trey stabbed his fingers into the bank of river earth to hoist himself upward and Kay did the same.

When they reached the top they rested against the tin wall of one of the bunkhouses with their faces tilted to the streaming rain and Trey closed his eyes to the torrential timpani beat that was music to his ears.

'Science,' he said to himself and suddenly he thought about Mum and Dad. He supposed they weren't killed because of him. They were killed despite him. Random, indiscriminate, just-because killings. He wasn't born bad; he was shown it and from that day on he knew the thing. For a while it was outside of him and then it pushed so hard he let it in.

He opened his eyes and saw that Kay had already paced the side of the building and he followed.

The rain fell heavy all around them and shrank clothes to skin, twisting and rinsing good life from their bones. They worked their way around the pitch-black yard and past the food tent that lay flat to ground like a lake and they had nothing much more than memory as guidance and occasionally they stopped and waited for the lightning to strike and spark their way.

They stood facing the porch of the farmhouse and Trey thought back to his first day and it seemed a long way back in the past. Time was like a daggered flash of light that caught the corner of his eye, something fleeting and then gone in a wrist flip.

Through the windows they could see the furniture had been pushed aside and Wilder's gang dangled from a party in full swing.

'Wilder's got no right to be in there,' said Kay and when a group of lads came on to the porch they ducked into the shadows.

'We need someplace to hide out,' said Trey.

'Over there,' said Kay and she pointed towards a broken-down truck across the track from the house. 'Come on.'

They ran with their heads bent to the ground and when they got to the vehicle Kay took her knife from her boot and she levered open the door.

'Haven't done that in a while,' she said as they climbed into the front seats.

'Spose you could get it started if you wanted.'

'Not this one. Broken down, init?'

'Spose.'

'You wanna try it? In case?'

'No, we don't need to draw more attention to us than we already got.' Trey watched her settle in behind the wheel and he wanted to ask her how she'd got messed up in the world but he kept his words half swallowed until suddenly they leapt out like a burp.

'Probably what you're guessin sittin there thinkin it.'

'I think a lot of things, don't mean I'm anglin.'

Kay looked at him and she twisted her face into a puzzle. 'You bin anglin a long time, don't deny it.'

'Well maybe a bit, I told you what I done, burnt down a barn and killed some horses.'

'You int said much bout before.'

'What you mean?'

'Bein in fosters and that.'

Trey shrugged and said he had no parents, which was the truth.

'Never had?'

'No I did, but they died when I was a boy.'

'I'm sorry to hear that.'

Kay looked at him and for a brief moment his life spun out of control, adrenalin cocktailed into something more; her up-close beauty cleared the sky of clouds and put stars into every corner of his eyes and it was then that he knew she saw the world the same.

'What bout your family?' he asked. 'What happened to em?'

Kay shook her head. 'Int nothin to tell. What bout your parents, you know how they died?'

Trey nodded. He wanted to tell her about the murders but in eight years he still hadn't found the words to say the thing out loud. Somehow that death evening didn't belong to him. He hadn't found a place in his past to have it make sense in the present.

Kay leant forward and wiped the steam from the window so they could keep an eye out for trouble and she told Trey that she had never met her father but she supposed he was out there somewhere and that her mother died of an overdose when she was thirteen.

'Sorry.'

'Don't be, it was three years ago. Anyway, she was a junkie bitch.'

There was a tone to her voice that ringed a big, black full stop.

191

Trey took out his lighter and flashed it between his knees and he brought it close to sizzle at the seams of his jeans as way of distraction because he wanted to ask about the scars on her back.

'Spose it int the past that matters so much as the future,' Trey said and looked across at her to see if there was a space for telling about Billy and the drawn-out revenge thing that at times had his flesh plucked from the inside out but her eyes had returned to the river-run world outside.

'I int got no future worth botherin,' she said.

'Course you have. Everyone got hopes of some kind.'

She looked at Trey and said she didn't.

'What's the point of livin if you int got no hope, no dreams, no nothin?'

'What's the point if you have? Nothin turns out how you want it in any case.'

Together they watched the storm grow crazy wild outside and Trey wondered about Kay and he wished he had something comforting to say but he did not.

'I wonder how long it would take for this truck to take float,' said Kay suddenly. 'We gonna wait till it comes through the floor?'

Trey sighed; the moment of honesty had come and gone. 'Spose it's now or never.'

He put his lighter back in his pocket and sat forward and he wiped the window clear with his sleeve. 'If we think this through what's the worst that can happen?'

'Wilder pops us with McKenzie's harpoon?' Kay opened the truck door and climbed out.

Through the front-room window they could see the party was heating up.

'Them lads gone back in?' asked Kay.

Trey nodded. 'Think so.'

'Let's go round the back.'

They sloped from the truck and crept on to the porch and edged around the farmhouse towards the back door.

'I'll go in first,' said Kay when she saw the kitchen light go off.

'You sure?' asked Trey.

'Bin here a couple times.' She stepped under the eaves and turned the handle. 'I got a funny feelin but we've committed now, int we?' She told him to stay close to the back door and to come and find her if he heard anything.

Trey stood by the door of the farmhouse and he kept his ear turned so he might hear danger. He dug his hands deep into the pockets of the oversized oilskin coat and wrapped it tight to keep the wet from rolling further than it already had and he tried to put his mind to something other than fear.

He looked up towards the sky and the stifling clouds that prowled there and suddenly he saw a star and then another push-pin point through the stuffing and something of that gap promised hope. A hole in the thick of it meant for breathing-thinking time; widening and kicking back the bullies to leave a sky full of stars, forever fields of fire wishes and promises combined.

Trey smiled and the bit of giddy that was in him had him think of Billy in good mind and he wondered if he saw those stars the same and he wished to heaven that he did; connecting dot to dots from one brother to another, a pattern coming and a pattern complete.

When the rain stopped fully he pulled down his hood and peeked into the kitchen for changing sound and he heard Wilder tell his boys that the celebration was on him.

'Them authorities int comin,' he shouted. 'Shit's gone down on the outside so them int botherin bout us and, what's more, look what I found in McKenzie's office.'

By the clink of metal against metal Trey knew he had found the master's keys.

They all cheered and Wilder told them it wouldn't be long now, not long until they could resume the work of the Preacher, it was just a matter of time. Trey wondered if Wilder truly believed that the camp was his. Perhaps a life in the Preacher's shadow really had made him crazy, his father so close and yet a million miles from what that should have meant.

He looked at the sky and the clouds that had returned to dampen his spirit and his heart sank suddenly and when he saw Kay appear through the kitchen dark the look across her face had it sink deeper.

'Follow me,' she said and Trey did as he was told.

They entered the house and went slow and they kept the music and grandstanding in mind because that meant Wilder and the others were still distracted and when Kay passed Trey the harpoon she'd found in the hallway he was glad to have it hooked crossways to his back.

He guided his hands both sides of the hall and he felt the soft velvet wallpaper that was comforting to his newly calloused hands and he stayed close to Kay with his heart flipping pinballs in his chest.

'You found the chaplain?' he whispered. 'Locked up in one of em upstairs rooms, is he?'

'No.' She went on into the dim hallway with Trey tailing and when she got to the corner door below the stairs she stopped.

She slid back the lock on the door and pulled it open and before they descended the cellar she turned to Trey with her eyes that said everything and nothing and told him to follow and to hold his nerve. There was something in the way she stopped suddenly that had him turn and think about heading back, but it was too late for bottling it now.

Silently they descended the stairs with the dancing kids punching dust-stars above their heads and Trey kept close to Kay for the fear of dark and enclosed space.

'Found the chaplain,' she said flatly when they reached the small damp room. When Trey didn't speak she said it again. She handed him the torch and told him to look because to look was to know what they were up against and Trey shone the light and in its glow he saw blood and beneath the blood he saw torture. A mass of welts and cuts and burns was etched into the chaplain's body, a horror story written in Braille.

'Check again,' he said and he watched Kay go to him and he saw her bend to search for pulse and breath but they both knew there was none.

Trey wrapped his arms around his ribs and he looked away and coughed the retch from him.

'You all right?' asked Kay.

Trey nodded.

'Wilder reckons the authorities int comin.' He looked at Kay and asked if she believed it.

'Reckon he's right, if what them saying bout the outside is true.'

'And that int all.'

'What?'

He looked Kay straight in the eye. 'It won't be long,' he continued. 'Won't be long till he finds em guns.'

They left the cellar and despite Trey's barely looking the imagery he saw there was in him good.

They went from the house and once out of sight they ran as fast as they could with the mud splashing them complete and Trey felt the moor that surrounded them snare him and pull him under.

'Christo!' screeched Lamby when he opened the door to them. 'What happened?'

'Everythin,' said Trey as he pushed past him. 'Get the fire goin, heat some water.'

'Boy, you need more'n a tip of water to clean you.'

'Just do it,' said Kay and she pushed him towards the dying fire.

'What you bin doin while we was gone?'

'Sleepin,' he smiled. 'So what happened? You find the chaplain?'

'Yes and no. Just get the fire goin, will you? And build it up good, we got things to discuss.'

Lamby knelt to the fire and he added enough wood to get it coming and he went to wake the twins and Trey heard him tell them that the shit had finally hit the fan.

Trey went to the dark corner of the stable to peel the sodden clothes from his back and he dried himself with a horse blanket and dressed in what spare clothes he had and all the time he couldn't get the image of the dead man out of his head.

He hung the blanket across his shoulders and took his sodden trainers to the fire and set them back from the flames and he sat to make the circle complete and he listened to Kay tell the three boys who were part baby what had happened in the farmhouse and he watched their expressions until realisation set in.

CHAPTER ELEVEN

The fire flames curled around the oddments of wood and peeped around corners and into holes like a lost thing.

Never before had Trey looked deep into a fire and not taken sanctuary there. Never had he looked for answers and found only questions in the black and the burn.

He listened to the others wind themselves into impossible knots and he had an inching instinct to go out all guns blazing but this small gang of ragtags had become something to him.

Their faces flashed ruby red in the fire light, reminding him of the kids in storybooks Mum used to read to him and Billy and he smiled remembering those fairy-tale stories that were close enough to the way things were now. Terror was everywhere he looked.

He leant back against the stall wall and looked across

at Kay and wished he could read her mind and he asked her what she was thinking.

'We need to keep one step ahead,' she shrugged. 'Think what Wilder might do next.'

'He's dangerous,' said Trey. 'That much we know.'

They all nodded.

'We gotta protect ourselves, int we?' Lamby stood up suddenly. 'Protect ourselves and defend the stables.'

'I'd rather escape,' said Trey and more than ever he wished he'd found a way before now to have done it.

'Who's for escapin?' he asked and he put up his hand and John and David did the same.

'Runnin away,' said Lamby.

'Int runnin, it's escapin, there's a difference.' Trey looked up at Lamby. 'Wilder's got McKenzie's keys and it int gonna take him long to work out which one opens the gun store, and when he does we've had it.'

Kay stood up and she shook the damp from her bones and she told him not to think about the fighting.

'Survival is what we gotta think about, survivin and then escape.'

Trey watched her get the rough stone she used for sharpening things and she spat on it and sliced her knife both sides across it.

'We're gonna make holes,' she shouted from the far end of the stable. 'Spyholes all sides in the wood so we can see things comin.'

'What kind of things?' asked Lamby.

'Anythin and everythin.'

They used what sharp poke tools they had to put holes where they could see tracks and kids heading their way and they drilled them high and stacked what they could to stand on.

'You know what we're doin?' said Lamby. 'We're buildin a castle. Wish we had hot tar and a portcullis.'

'We got the harpoon,' said Kay. 'It's good for what we need it for.'

'And I'm gonna sharpen sticks,' decided Lamby. 'Never know when you might need a pointy stick.'

'Spears,' said Trey.

'What?'

'Call em spears; nobody ever went to battle with a pointy stick.'

'You can call em what you want if you help me.'

Trey took the knife and he went and sat with Lamby and his sticks while the others secured the fortress.

'You worried?' asked Lamby.

'Course.'

'You reckon Wilder got more killin to do?'

Trey shrugged. 'Don't think about it.'

'Can't stop.'

Trey couldn't stop thinking about it either. The image of the chaplain slumped and bloody was the only thing he saw when he closed his eyes.

'Let's just do what we got planned.'

They sharpened broom poles and sticks into lethal weapons and the ends of two metal mop handles were hammered all ways into star points.

'We're plannin to go into battle,' said Lamby.

'Protection is all.'

'Spose. But sometimes you get beat enough times in life you start to wonder what it's like to do the beatin.' Lamby gathered up his stash of sticks and went to show Kay like a kid with a crap class-made gift.

Through the night and into first light they worked at securing the stables into half a chance of survival and when there was nothing left to do but wait David put five potatoes into the hot embers of the fire for breakfast and in time one potato each was what they had.

At full light Lamby couldn't keep himself away from standing on the crates at the hole near the door and he rested his face against the wood with one eye closed and a steel spear in his hand.

'If anyone dares come I got em, don't you worry.'

'We int worried,' said Kay.

'Good cus don't be.'

'Maybe we'll all go nappin and leave you to it,' said Trey.

Lamby moved back from the hole. 'Really?'

'I'm messin with you.' Trey made a face at the twins across the dying fire and they all laughed.

'Not so funny,' said Lamby as he peeped through the hole. 'Cus we got trouble brewin.'

Kay jumped up next to him. 'Wilder's on his way,' she shouted.

'Kay!' came the shouts when Wilder reached the shade of the stable walls. 'Rudeboy, where you at?'

'Who's askin?' shouted Lamby through the peep hole and he couldn't hide his delight in asking it.

'Stop messin me, blow-boy. Where they at?'

'I'll see if they're in.'

Trey told Lamby to stop winding more than was necessary and he unlocked the top half of the stable door and rested the harpoon on the ledge towards the square of marching boy soldiers.

'See you found my weapon,' said Wilder. 'Spose that means you came snoopin round the farmhouse last night.'

'Think you'll find it was the master's,' Trey said.

'Well I'm the master now.'

'Is that right?'

'That's the truth and you know it.'

'Why you here, Wilder?'

'You got someplace other to go? Thinkin of escapin perhaps?'

'Maybe.'

'Well don't bother cus we got this place surrounded.'

Trey looked back into the two shadow corners of the stable at the twins pressed steadfast like rivets holding up the timber walls and they both turned and nodded.

'So?' Trey asked. He was feeling nervous, hot with the possibility of battle.

'So we can keep you locked up or we can flush you out, just lettin you know where you stand.'

'On my own two feet is where I stand.'

'So you int gonna change your mind?'

'Bout what?'

'Becomin one of me boys. The others can stay put mind.'

Trey pretended to laugh despite his punching heart and he told him never ever in a million years. It felt good to be doing the right thing now the demon had gone.

'Well now that's a real shame cus I know we two got a lot in common.'

'I int got nothin in common with you,' said Trey.

'What your little friends wouldn't give for a bit of backstory.'

'Shut it, Wilder.'

'My dad, your dad, who killed who and all that.'

'What's he talkin bout?' asked Kay.

'I know the Preacher told you it was an accident or such.'

Trey didn't know what to say and he kept his mouth closed for thinking time.

'There int nothin like war between kinfolk, is there, Trey? Two men with some same blood pumpin, battlin, fightin, the one gun goin off and then one's dead and one's alive.'

'What you sayin?' Trey asked.

'Must be hard is all.'

'He said he dint shoot nobody.'

Wilder started to laugh and Trey wanted to bury him where he stood.

'It's the Preacher we're talkin bout. You reckon you're gonna believe a mean bastard like that?'

'Just leave us alone, Wilder,' shouted Kay. 'Leave us be and we'll leave you the same.'

Wilder stubbed his fat-foot boots wide in the earth. 'I would if I could, but there's one small problem and that's the chaplain. Maybe if you kept your meddlin noses out last night then maybe this would be a whole different mornin.'

'You killed him,' said Kay flatly.

'He asked for it.' He started to laugh and he made sure his gang of dumb lads did the same.

'You're a liar,' said Trey and he lifted the harpoon and rubbed his finger against the trigger. 'How's this gonna end?' he asked.

Wilder stood with hands on hips, his knuckles waist-wormed into the sides of his belly and he kicked at the puddle at his feet and he told them that this was in no way over and he looked at Trey and asked him to give his regards to his brother.

'You int got no right,' shouted Trey.

'I'm just helpin you see sense is all. Dad was a liar on most accounts, you can take that as a given.'

Trey passed the harpoon to Kay and unlocked the lower part of the door. The two boys eyed each other with disdain and Trey could feel the blood that was in him turn from simmer to boiling.

'I thought we'd make somethin of you soon enough,' continued Wilder as he turned to go. 'Somethin more'n your daddy's weaklin boy anyway.'

Trey felt the shame of cowardice steam from him, he couldn't let the boy speak to him like this, he stepped forward.

'I int no coward,' he shouted and he felt his lungs fill with hot air.

'What's that?'

He saw Wilder turn on his heels and Trey called him back into the noose of jackal kids and he felt the heat return to his blood and combust into flames. It split open and into that ravine he poured his anger and frustration and he channelled it if not towards the Preacher then his son.

He ran after Wilder and thumped him in the chest and it was a shock to both of them.

They stood for a one-two second, two boys resembling and struggling with their disappointing past. When fighting came it struck with a blur of punches and they slotted neatly into the gaps where words should have been.

Trey knew there was only one place left for saving face and this was it, violence for violence's sake. He didn't mind the pain so much; it made him feel closer in some way to those that were dead, closer to Billy. The hurt brought him to them, brought him nearer to what he should have felt. He was lucky, he had lived, but Trey knew there was no luck in lonely.

It felt good to fight in any case, have everything in him that was pent and stifled and bent wrong come out with the burn of power and hurt.

He saw faces circle and the chants of glee stuffed his ears and he was glad to reveal something of himself for the first time.

The damn thing wrong was the fight was over too soon and Trey stood ripped from his prey with blood spilt everywhere about him and he heard himself promise the boy that this was not the end but the start of something big and he realised that by his own tongue he had declared war.

When Kay aimed the harpoon at Wilder and asked him to leave or else, the gang took her threat seriously and despite Wilder's shouting and threatening he joined the others and made his way back towards the horizon.

'What's Wilder talkin bout?' asked Lamby when they entered the stables. 'Bout your family and that?'

'Nothin,' said Trey and he felt his hands go numb with the squeeze of anger.

'What's that bout a brother?'

'Leave it,' shouted Kay and she grabbed Lamby's arm and pulled him away.

Trey felt like he was standing at the edge of battle and then he sat where he stood and the memory of demon filled his ears with screams steeped in hellfire language. He closed his eyes and out of necessity he went back to boy a moment and he crouched inside the cupboard dark and peeping and he set himself a scene and waited. Through pain and suffering he forced memory to seek and search and he saw Mum the way he didn't like and he saw the Preacher stand over her and he went back to the bang bang and maybe he saw the gun and the stranger, the other man who stood before. Maybe the Preacher was right, maybe definitely he was right.

Trey opened his eyes and pushed the tears dry and he told himself to trust his memory just this once. He got up and went to the others and he told them not to bother asking what he couldn't explain and he joined them in sitting.

'Does this mean we won the battle?' asked Lamby. 'With you whackin him and all.'

'No it don't,' said Kay. 'He'll be back soon enough and he'll bring some kind of cracked plan with him.'

'Let him try,' said Lamby and he flipped his spear from one hand to the next and he smiled at Trey and Trey saw fear buried beneath the bravado.

'We should be ready for him,' said Kay. 'More than ready.'

'Like how?' asked Trey. 'Can't do much more than tool up and wait.'

David started to draw with a stone on the concrete floor.

'Set traps,' shouted Lamby and he pointed to what it was being drawn. 'We need string or wire and things to tie to it, jingly things and things that clank, whatever.'

They poked about the stable to collect forgotten cans and broken tack and Trey went outside to kick about the perimeter with the harpoon hugging his shoulder. He toed the roundabout rubble and picked over the bones of a discarded engine until the bucket he carried was rim full with the clank of unusable useful things.

They tied the bits and bobs on to rope thinned to string and strung them out like childish clothes lines low to the ground.

'Put em where you think they'll come sneakin,' said Lamby. 'Not just tracks but between. That'll catch em out.'

The four boys went about the slow-drying sludge earth while Kay stood guard with the harpoon. She looked tired and beat and Trey felt tired and beat the same. The sun had returned momentarily and it bit hard and Trey could feel the heat push through his T-shirt and burn his eyes as he scanned the horizon for signs of life. He glanced at Kay and went to stand next to her.

'You all right?' she asked.

Trey nodded.

'You don't have to say nothin but I'm here in any case.'

'I know,' he tried to smile and he thanked her.

'How long you think?' he asked.

Kay shrugged and said Wilder and his gang would be back before long. 'You did punch him.'

'I mean everythin, how long till we escape or Wilder goes crazy?'

She looked at him and she didn't answer because what was there to say.

'It's like a nightmare,' he said.

Kay nodded. 'Just keeps gettin worse.'

'What they did to the chaplain.'

'Don't think about it.'

'Can't stop.'

They watched the lads and they were kids out playing on a summer's day, stringing up the lengths of buckled metal like they were putting up bunting for a party.

'I feel almost responsible for them three,' said Trey. 'Stupid, I know.'

Kay stood close and he could feel the stick of sweat on her arm glue to his. 'It int stupid,' she said. 'Them there are more like kids than us. Maybe they saw more of childhood to know it.'

'The twins are tryin to tell me somethin,' shouted Lamby. 'They've got an idea.'

They went into the stables and crouched to the stable floor.

'Forget that,' said Kay. 'Go snap more planks for the fire.'

Trey said he'd get the wood and he noticed Kay had filled one of the metal buckets brimful with water and he watched as she settled it central to the fire and he knew what it might be used for and he hated knowing it.

'The twins are drawin the camp,' said Lamby when Trey brought the wood to the fire. 'Somethin that might be useful, so far we know it's upstairs of a bunkhouse.'

'Which one?' asked Trey.

'Lynner house, they drew girls.'

'The chaplain's office?'

'Looks like it.'

Trey stood and watched as the brothers fought over the different stones they used to chalk the picture and Kay stopped what she was doing to listen.

'Somethin with knobs,' giggled Lamby. 'Somethin lecko?'

The boys nodded.

'A radio?' he shouted.

The boys shrugged. Yes and no.

'A radio that's not a radio,' said Lamby. 'You got me stumped there, boys. Has it got somethin to do with science?'

John drew a telephone next to the radio and the others asked questions until Kay finally nailed it.

'A CB radio,' she said. The boys grinned with delight.

'Thought they just existed in films,' said Trey. 'Dint think they was a thing.'

'Used em to talk to aliens, dint they?' asked Lamby. 'That would be somethin, wouldn't it?'

'You know this for sure?' Kay asked the twins. 'You seen it?'

The boys nodded and she believed them and she said they saw more than most because people thought them stupid.

'They're just dumb,' said Lamby. 'No not dumb, just don't speak.'

They decided that the twins would go and look for the radio because they were unobtrusive. They took the knife and a sack and one of the metal spears and everyone wished them luck.

'Good boys, int they?' said Lamby. 'Our little soldier twins. Best thing is nobody takes much notice of em. Bet Wilder don't even know their names.'

'If they find the CB radio and it works that'd be somethin,' said Kay.

'What?' asked Lamby.

'Maybe we got a chance, contact the Army Police, tell em somebody's bin killed. They gotta listen then.'

Trey had a little worry scratching at his insides and he picked at his fingers and fiddled with everything and nothing much. He thought about Billy alone out there somewhere and he thought about his funny homemade family and he worried about them all the same and he wondered if things would ever get back to normal.

The three of them took turns to keep watch at the hole in the door and although nobody said it each thought about the passing of time since they'd last seen the boys.

When it was Trey's turn to stand guard he remembered where the sun had been earlier in the sky and he saw it was now greased in a cloudy midday smear and he guessed that maybe two hours had come and gone. He closed his eyes and walked the twins through the camp, allowing them time for hiding and creeping, and he wondered if one hour there and one hour back was about right. Two hours to make a fifteen-minute round trip, maybe it was about right, it had to be.

He kept guard longer than his allocated shift and drank the last of the tin-cup tea somebody passed to him with his eyes fixed in the direction of camp. He could imagine the twins' heads bobbing, faces smiling, the hessian sack heavy in their hands, job done. He looked at other things besides and told himself that it didn't matter what time they returned because it was his understanding that if you didn't care about something then it happened and if you did then it didn't.

He finished the tea and flicked the dregs at the ground and still the twins didn't come.

'You see anythin?' shouted Kay. 'You see the boys yet?'

'Nothin,' he said. 'No change 'cept the rain's back. You'd think we were the only survivors left out here.'

'Out here in the middle,' said Lamby as he stepped up beside him. 'Hey,' he shouted, 'I think I see somethin.'

'What you see that I dint?' Trey moved forward.

'Movement, I swear it.'

'Don't say you see somethin if it int true.'

'Look, someone's comin.'

'What you mean, someone?' Trey pushed him aside and watched as the solitary figure approached.

'Who is it?' asked Kay.

'It's David, he's on his own.'

'What's he doin?' asked Lamby.

'He's runnin.'

David sped up and over the ridge with a lifetime of pic-'n'-mix words bursting from his mouth. He ran and he fell and he pulled himself up despite his legs that had gone to mush and his shouting was rough and ragged and wrong. They stood with their hearts in their mouths and built the rubble of sounds into words and Kay opened the door for him to aim at.

'Look behind him,' shouted Lamby. 'Whole world's headin our way.'

Trey jumped from the platform and he passed the harpoon to Lamby and they stood battle ready with the spears fierce in their hands.

The water in the metal bucket boiled in the belly of the fire and they let it pop and hiss as David jumped the traps and sprinted towards the door with the enemy closing in like storm clouds over the horizon.

'Where's John?' shouted Kay when he was in earshot.

David fell through the door and they could see he was rag-soaked from head to toe in blood and mud and the metallic tang made Trey retch. He swallowed and made a cough out of his heaving.

'Dead,' said David and the word stuck to the air like gum.

'They killed a twin,' shouted Lamby. 'The twins int twins no more.'

Twenty plus boys and girls came running and when they were close some hit the traps and fell and the rest stood awkward all round.

'Where's Wilder?' shouted Kay.

'He said to send his apologies,' shouted an older boy, his mouthpiece.

'What the hell he do?' shouted Lamby. 'What the hell he do to the twins?'

Trey let one hand drop from the spear and he linked it into Lamby's arm a moment.

'They was snoopin,' said the boy. 'Wilder don't like snoopers. Found em pokin in the chaplain's office and int nobody allowed in there.'

'What happened?' asked Kay.

The boy shrugged and Trey tried to place him and he thought maybe he worked in the slaughterhouse.

'Fightin's what happened.'

Trey could no longer stomach the everyday talking and asking. The fire inside him was so unexpected that it almost pushed him sideways.

'You kill John?' he shouted.

The boy flipped another up-down shrug.

'You killed one brother and you're after the other one. Is that how it goes?' he stepped forward despite Kay telling him to keep back.

'It was his own fault,' said the boy.

'You bastard.'

'Got himself killed, dint he.'

'What you talkin bout?'

'They was snoopin, wouldn't say why and then some of the lads took up chase and whichever one of em dopey lads got fried.'

'Ran into the fence,' shouted some scrag-tag girl. 'Everybody knows them volts is as high as they can go.'

'How we know to believe you?' asked Kay.

'Cus why lie?'

'So why you here?' asked Trey. 'You plannin on finishin off the other one?' He closed another five, six steps between them and held the spear close to the boy's belly.

'You wouldn't,' said the boy, reading Trey's mind. 'You just wouldn't.'

'How you know that, I mean really?'

'Cus you int got no guts for blood, lads in butchers told me, you're a pussy.'

'Is that right?'

'No smarts to you either.'

'How's that?'

'Cus if you did you'd be standin on this side of things.'

Trey laughed and he clenched the spear between his fingers. 'Smart thing is standin gainst you, idiot, not sidlin and runnin with the pack.'

The boy shrugged and said, 'Whatever.'

Trey would have left things spiking and rattling between them if it wasn't for that 'whatever' and he leant to push the spear just a little into the boy's stomach.

'Trey,' shouted Kay. 'Actin like them don't solve nothin, leave it.'

Trey lunged a heartbeat one two into the boy's belly but when he saw the ring of blood colouring the fabric of his shirt he pulled back.

Trey knew he was shouting, his mouth snapping open and shut like a barking dog, and despite Kay's arms tightening around his waist he could feel the inner bomb that was fire finally explode.

Kay had him tipped back on to the ground and she was shouting at him and she called him an idiot but he knew this already.

The boy looked at Trey with fear waxed into place like a mannequin, 'so what' and 'whatever' knitted into his brow.

'You don't even care,' said Trey and he must have shouted it because the mess of argument quietened and everybody looked at him. He stared into the boy's eyes and shouted it over and over and he wanted to ask why but all he got in reply was, *Whatever, whatever, whatever.*

Lamby pulled Trey to his feet and the injured boy was lifted and dangled back towards enemy lines and as they retreated Kay shouted after them that it was nothing more than a scratch and they were quits on all things.

Inside the stable Trey sat by the fire for the warmth and he bunched so close he could feel his skin pucker and coil in the heat.

'You're shiverin,' said Lamby and he wrapped a blanket snug across Trey's shoulders. 'I'll make sweet tea with the bag I've bin savin and the rest of the sugar. Sugar for shock, that's what they say, init?'

Trey watched him go to fill the pan with water and asked where the bucket of boiling water had gone.

Lamby looked up and grinned. 'Used it. Cupped a good bit bout with a mug, splashed them buggers enough that they'll think me more'n a skinny runt.'

'Why you laughin?' asked Trey. 'I nearly killed a boy and you're laughin like we bin on a jolly.'

Lamby shrugged and there was a bit of the 'whatever' about him that had Trey grab him by the collar. 'I could've killed a boy, you got that? Killed him and they killed one of our own maybe and the chaplain definitely and here you are all smiles and giggles.'

'I int laughin,' said Lamby, tears pooling in his eyes.

'Let him go,' said Kay and she crouched to prise his fingers from Lamby's shirt.

They watched the boy run from the stables and into the storm-eye and there was nothing they could shout to get him back. They sat in the quiet except for David who called out for his brother in the stall beside them and when tea was made they held on to its comfort as long as possible.

'He'll just sit round the back a minute.' She looked at Trey. 'I know you int OK so I won't ask, but you'll get a bit of yourself back soon enough.'

'You don't know that,' he said and he looked at her through the lift of heat. 'How you know that?'

Kay shook her head and she kicked off her boots and socks and stretched her muddy feet towards the fire.

'How you know a thing like that?' he asked again. 'How you know what it's like to lose it enough to come close to puttin someone in the dirt, someone you don't know and who done nothin to you besides.'

Kay sighed and settled her mug of tea in her lap and she looked at him and looked into the fire and sighed again.

'What?' he asked.

'You know how you spend your life runnin from somethin and the faster and further you go the closer it gets you inside?'

'Like a growin thing?'

'And it sticks to you in a wrap-around way no matter what, like strings of elastic, snappin and trippin you over.'

'Is that how life's got you?'

Kay looked at him and shrugged. 'Spose. You gotta find a way to live with the things you've done, int no other way.'

'Kay,' he asked, 'what happened after your mum died? Fosters was you?'

'Not quite.'

'What then?'

'Did my own thing, knockin bout the streets and whatever.'

'Nobody bother to track you down? The social and all that?'

Kay started to laugh. 'Couldn't keep up with me, could they. I had a knack for runnin invisible, for a time anyway.'

'What happened?'

'Got caught is what happened, joined a gang, and I spose they weren't the most inconspicuous gang in the world.' She looked at Trey and he guessed she could see the confusion on his face.

'Stealin cars, robbin village stores.' She shrugged. 'And I won't say it weren't fun cus it was but all good things gotta come to an end.'

'You got caught?'

'I killed-someone got caught.'

Trey kept his eyes on her for the flicker that might have meant funning but by the look in her eyes he could see she wasn't.

'What happened?'

'The lad was in a rival gang. He was a mean bastard.'

Trey shook his head. 'Is that why you're in here for so long?'

Kay looked at him and he could see tragedy was setting up stall.

'Two years and countin,' she said and he could see her pain and he knew it now more than ever because he felt it the same.

'It's funny,' she continued. 'Until recently I used to dream of escape and now that maybe there's a chance, dunno, I'm not so sure.'

'What you mean?' asked Trey.

'Where would I go? What would I do? This place is as close to home as I've ever known.' She looked at Trey and shrugged. 'As I said, I int got no dreams, there int no master plan for me.'

'How'd you kill him?' asked Trey.

'Knocked him down during a fight, things were gettin hairy, we had to make a quick getaway. Dint mean to, thought he'd be OK so I left him.' She shook her head remembering. 'Saw him sat in the road in the rear view, just sittin there he was.'

She pulled her knees up to her chin and told him not to worry in any case. 'We all done things. Each damn kid in this hole done things, bad things. Don't make you bad all the way through.'

Trey downed his tea despite it being too hot and he crouched to pour himself another. He wanted to know more of that inner steel coil that was Kay's core and he wanted her to feed him blunt truths all night through. To know other stories made them just that, stories. 'David's quiet,' he said.

'Sleepin, hope so anyway.'

'What you reckon bout him?'

'I'd say he's our biggest concern.'

'You think somethin's snapped in him that we can't fix?'

'Yep.'

Trey nodded. 'I do too.'

'I think he's gonna wake at first light with enough charge in him to get up, unlock that door and go out revenging. Someone else gonna get killed either way.'

'Wish he'd say somethin bout what happened,' said Trey. 'Funny all those words comin in a jumble and then gone, just like that.' He wondered if Wilder would use the radio to call for backup of some kind, maybe he'd contact the Preacher, but Trey knew he was long gone.

'He might try use it, but then he's havin a ball right now. Wouldn't wanna ruin the one thing he's always wanted,' said Kay.

'Power,' they said in unison.

When it was time for guard duty Kay went to the back of the stables and Trey went to the front and he propped himself against the wall. He stood with one foot on the other and each foot took turns to rest but still they ached and sat stiff in the trainers that were split and flapping and more useless than useful. Outside in the diminishing light the rain fell in iron-sheet drifts and the fierce wind picked up everything not bolted down and flung it towards freedom.

Trey thought about his day in a spin and the pinpoint thing settling central was that he knew what it was to harbour such blistering heat that he could have killed a boy.

'He was a criminal,' he said to himself. 'He was a criminal the same as all of us, it wouldn't've mattered.'

He said this but he didn't believe it and he knew that if he had taken the boy's life something of his own would have gone down with it. The demon would have returned.

He shuffled his standing and continued to watch the rain transform the moor into an ocean running rivers. He thought about boats and escape and a passage flowing to the sea and his fantasy sailed the four of them around the world but mostly it sailed him and brother Billy towards that alternative world of fantasy where they would be happy.

Through the drifting rain the moor played games in a constant shift of shape. Things that were there weren't and things that were crept like shadows beneath the radar of continual looking. That was how it was with the thin flap outline of movement worrying the horizon. Something was present in the lightning flash that hinted and beat the heart, something that was and then wasn't.

Trey stood with both feet planted and waited for the next spark of electricity to smack and he was afraid to blink and miss the thing approaching. He kept his eyes on the one spot in the black and when the momentary light was tripped he saw it and had it trapped in mind. When he closed his eyes he still saw it, a photographic image of someone getting closer.

'Someone's comin,' he said to himself and then he shouted it and he looked across at Kay and beckoned her over.

'Should I open the door?' he asked. 'Open the door for a better look.'

'Not yet.' Kay climbed up next to him. 'It might be a trap.' She stood close to the spyhole and when she couldn't see anything she decided to venture outside.

'I tell you I saw somethin,' said Trey.

'I believe you.'

She unbolted the top door with the harpoon in hand and scanned one way and then the other and Trey wondered if he had seen anything at all when suddenly Kay said she could see someone. 'They're wavin,' she said. 'Who the hell would be wavin?'

They stood jammed within the door frame and watched the moving space that pushed the rain into an outline of a figure and they waited.

'They're shoutin somethin,' said Trey and they listened until words formed familiar sounds. 'They're sayin your name,' he said to Kay. 'It's Lamby.'

They waited for him to run the final stretch and stood aside when he lurched towards them.

'What the hell,' said Trey. 'Where you bin?'

'I can't …' Lamby held his stomach and they waited for him to catch his breath.

'You're an idiot,' said Trey. 'You could've got yourself killed.'

'I thought you'd be pleased?' He looked at Trey and Trey felt bad and looked away.

They sat at the fire while the dishevelled Lamby told them about his midnight meandering and what he'd seen through his wandering about camp.

'The main gate's guarded by some tooled-up kids,' he said. 'But the towers are clear.'

'You heard if anyone gonna come for us?' asked Kay.

Lamby shook his head. 'Anyway the best bit is all the leccy's bin taken out.'

'A power cut?' asked Trey.

'Lightnin, took the whole lot out.' He smiled proudly at his discovery. 'Means we can escape now, don't it? Now the fence int on.'

Trey nodded and he looked at his friend and told him that he had something to say to him and that was sorry.

'For what?'

'For goin at you.'

Lamby shrugged. 'Spose you'd just lost it. I should have known to stay back, I could see the wilds in you.'

224

Trey could picture himself in his friend's eyes, caught in a moment of fear-fight.

A looked-after kid with nobody to tell him how to step away, lose face. He was the Preacher and Wilder and Dad all boiled into one, a boy with a forever fire fury in his belly and fear in his heart, self-destruction from the inside out. His first social worker had told him he had devil blood running through him, and then everyone started saying it. It was the fire thing that had them think it, made them recognise the one mean demon within.

He got up and went to be alone with the shame that was coming, and would always be, and he tried to fix it with hope but there was no room left inside for wishing.

He leant over the half-door and watched light filter slowly through the low-slung drizzle, today's pain and despair consigned to yesterday, to history.

He saw Mum standing outside and she was dressed in the veil of vapour and she smiled at him and nodded her pride and it was then that Trey knew he had done right by certain things. In all ways he had tried right and she told him that there was one more thing he had to do and Trey knew this already because it was in his heart. He was nothing like Wilder, he knew this now.

'You gonna be all right, son.' She smiled through the haze and Trey nodded and he joined her in happiness because this was the last time he would see her and he knew this was good. Reality had replaced fantasy and he could feel the space of an uncluttered mind stretch to new possibilities as the vision of Mum thinned to wind and just rain.

'It's gonna be OK,' he said to himself and then he said it out loud for everyone to hear because he didn't just hope it so but he believed it over and over again. If he still had it in him he could save his friends and more certain than that he would save Billy.

CHAPTER TWELVE

The decision to head out under cover of darkness was the only sensible option left open to them and as soon as Trey said it to the others they knew it was the right thing to do. They bundled what was needed into tight cloth sacks and each one of them had something to carry and a weapon or spear of sorts in their arms.

'What about the horses?' asked Lamby.

'I'm gonna let em go,' said Kay. 'Give em a bit of a chance at least. Int like we're gonna return.'

They opened the stable doors and smacked the horses out into the open and they watched them run and could hear them whinny and giggle in the dark.

Kay took the key and locked the door out of habit and into the unknown they marched.

They walked the fence in single file and went fast in the hope that they would not be seen and they tailed it like a guideline to freedom. Once they had distance on their side they could stop and cut and peel the fence.

The dark blue haze of foetal night curled itself around them and it gathered them close and gave them courage.

'I'm gonna touch the fence,' said Lamby laughing. 'I'm gonna defo touch it.'

Trey looked at him and told him to take their escape seriously.

'I am. Come on, Trey. I'll do it if you do it.'

David looked at him and at the fence in a passing flash and his eyes soon swung back to digging the bit of earth in front of him.

'I'm gonna do it.'

'Do it then!' shouted Kay.

'I'm scared, you do it.'

Kay threw down her bag and the harpoon and she checked that all the lights were off and then she stood at the perimeter and she rubbed her hands together and planted them into the fence.

'Nothin,' she said. 'Now shut up.'

They snaked low to the bogland while pushing forward and there were places that were waterlogged in the deep and they had to double back.

Trey stayed at the tail end of their line to keep one eye on Lamby and the other on David. Just to know the grieving boy was walking was something. Trey knew well how slow a heart could beat in guilt and grief, barely moving, not wanting to move but for the slow flow of blood passing through. He looked up into the sky above them. The clouds bumped black and they split white where moonlight won and he wished for rain; if the rain came back they'd have a little more cloak in which to hide. The dark horizon trickled light in a run and the colours snagged in the shadow trees and tors in a loop around them. The morning would be upon them before they knew it and it would hit them like a spotlight.

'We int got long,' he said. 'Not long till mornin.'

'We're fine,' said Kay. 'It's still early.'

'We could go faster,' suggested Lamby 'Could try anyway.'

'We're goin as fast as we can, considerin the slop we're walkin through,' said Kay

'If we went faster our feet wouldn't sink so far into the mud,' he continued.

Kay stopped and pointed the torch at Lamby and shook her head.

'They wouldn't,' he said.

'Yes they would.'

'It's science, they wouldn't.'

'You can't just make stuff up and call it science,' said Trey. 'Sayin somethin don't make it true.'

'Well I know it's true, read it so.'

Trey told him to keep moving and he watched his step and used his spear as a walking stick and at times he stopped to scan the shadow horizon for the bounce of enemy heads. His brain felt crushed at the temples and his body ached.

Slowly they were sinking into a lake of mud where the rain had fallen and streamed towards the fence and they tried desperately to wade through it. Trey felt the last remnants of his trainers peel from his feet.

It was then that he thought about what it might be like to climb the fence instead of cutting it, run at the razor wire and pitch over, and he was about to suggest it when Lamby said he could hear something.

'What is it?' whispered Kay.

'Somethin,' he said.

They crouched low within the bog and went on bent and buckled until Kay stopped suddenly.

'You hear that?'

'Wilder?' asked Lamby.

'Keep quiet.'

'If it is we gotta run.'

They slumped down in the mud but Trey felt Lamby pull from the mire and head blindly towards exposed land and they heard him fall headlong into another gully.

'Gotcha,' someone shouted in the distance.

'Gotcha all.' Kay flashed the torch towards Wilder standing on firm ground behind them.

'Silly kids,' he laughed. 'Bin waitin for you.'

Trey looked up and in the torchlight he could see Anders coming towards them with Lamby cat's-cradled in a rope behind him.

'Catch a fox and put em in a box,' he laughed.

'Get lost, Anders,' shouted Kay. 'Let the boy go.'

'Ah don't be like that,' said Wilder and he stuck out a hand to pull her from the suck and she ignored it.

'Where you think you're goin in any case? Merry band of misfits.'

Kay used her spear to hitch herself free. 'Just let Lamby go. Let him go and we'll keep quits on all this.'

Trey tried to ignore their shouting so he could concentrate on wiggling his toes towards solid ground and he kept himself steady with the metal spear hidden sideways in the slop. He watched Kay stand firm and when Wilder made a grab for her Trey put both hands round the spear to spring free of the bog and he went at Wilder in a charge because the boy was everything that he was not. They fell to the ground and Trey grabbed his neck and he shook him and he punched him black with muck and bruise. The world around them fell away in a tumble; brick by brick it crumbled and its fabric became worthless dust, brutal fighting turning what was some measure of right and wrong into rubble.

Shouting and screaming spilt out on to the moor and it was comrade and enemy and Trey heard his own voice add to the sound of thumping and kicking. A fireball spiralled in his gut and had him bound to Wilder, two boys mirrored in mud and blood and nothing but the whites of their eyes flashing silver daggers in the dark until finally they fell apart.

'Trey!' shouted Kay. 'Leave him. Anders stabbed Lamby.' Trey was slow to get to his feet, the sudden weight of reality holding him down, the scene another dream or familiar nightmare returned, and he waited until some part of his old self came back. He stood and watched the scene around him unfold; David standing with the harpoon at Anders' head and Wilder in the background, running and threatening gunfire.

'I'll be back,' he shouted. 'I'll make a promise of that. Gonna get me a gun and take you down, boom.'

Kay told David to let Anders go and to give her the harpoon and when the enemy was out of earshot she told them to carry the thin, brittle boy up to higher ground so they could keep lookout.

'He's bleedin bad,' said Trey. 'Harpoon went straight through and out the other side, I don't know what's bin got and what int.'

They sat on a small rise of land to keep watch while Kay bathed Lamby's wound with a little of the bottled drinking water and she soaked rags and put pressure on his stomach and they all sat dumbfounded, lost in collective trance.

Trey felt blood running in and out and all about him and he looked at Kay and saw the same.

'This int right,' he said.

'Brave or stupid?' she asked. 'That's what I'm wonderin.'

'What you mean?'

'Standing up to Wilder. Maybe it would have been easier to go along with the crowd.'

Trey shook his head. 'But that int you, is it.'

'No, but I wish sometimes it was.'

'That's a bad cut on your head.'

'Same as all of us.'

'Still runnin blood, let me clean it.'

Trey dipped a rag into the water and he held it to her forehead and wiped it clean and he soaked it and rinsed and told her to hold it there a minute. For a moment he wished for Kay's strength, she was sorted in all the ways that he was not. He wanted to be like her, become the hero, have her in his life in the way he knew he never would.

'Spose we can't go back,' he said. 'No point in any case.'

He turned to David and it was as if he was a newly moulded brother and he smiled and the boy did the same.

'You all right?' he asked.

David shook his head. 'Lamby gone die,' he said.

'No he int,' said Trey. 'Will take more'n a stab wound to keep him down.' He nodded as if in agreement with his own words and he accepted David's speech as if today was always going to be the day for it.

'Lamby'll be OK,' he said.

'Doctor, is you?' asked Kay.

'Don't be daft, it's just –'

'What?'

'He'd be dead by now.'

'Int much comfort in thinkin bout death either way,' she said and she continued to bandage Lamby with what surplus clothing they had.

Trey sighed. 'When you think Wilder will make his final move?'

'Soon, once he gets the guns, that'll be it. Game over. We gotta go.' Kay looked at him for the longest time with those eyes that said a million things but not to him. 'While it's still dark, we gotta go no matter what and keep on goin.'

'I know,' said Trey and he smiled to make it all right and he said it again. They had to keep going, they had to escape camp. Sitting there in the middle of nowhere he could feel the loose weightless cords unravelling all around him.

He could smell the damp ash sting of fires gone over and the acrid tang of burning rubber and he imagined the gangs of kids throwing the redundant detritus of a once-was society into the pyre with manic glee. He wasn't the only pyro-boy on the block any more, they were all fire-starters now, all had aspects of destruction and chaos sparking in their veins, going through them like a dose of volts.

'It's a slow death now, init, just sittin here? A long time waitin and a slow death waitin to happen.' Whether through starvation or a knife to the throat, they were kids standing in line to be tipped head first into an early grave.

He looked at Kay and at her battle scars and rags and aged eyes that told more than a lifetime of horrors and hurts and not just in the last few days.

Still, there was some hope in those eyes that shared a destiny of some kind and he could have cried for them. He wished he had a way to know the right thing to do, but Trey knew only one option remained and that was escape. To find a way out of the camp was to save his friends and go save Billy and only then would he be able to equal things out with the world and maybe even save himself.

'I've got it.' He stood up and dug his bare feet dead into the ground. 'I know how we might get out.'

'OK,' said Kay and she pointed the light towards Lamby and then she said it again.

Together they lifted him on to David's back and in single file they went out into that which was as unknown as anything they'd ever known. The smell of fire was everywhere apparent and Trey could see them burn clearly as they reached higher ground.

Tiny pockets of movement making something out of nothing in the dark. His heart wanted to go to them, always he wanted to return to fire, to have it in his eyes and throat and pull it down into his gut, that rolling power of heat and danger never left him, it never forgot him either.

They went as fast as circumstance allowed, stepping with quick tiptoe flicks as if the earth was a run of boiling lava, testing it with every step over and over again.

Trey held his spear in a light grip and he thought about camp and what it meant to those who knew it and what it meant to those who did not. Either way nobody could have imagined this.

'You know which way we're headin?' Kay asked.

'Bit. I know where rough in daylight and that's enough.'

The dark night called out to the storm and turned it into its accomplice and together they tripped and tricked the gang of four until everything blurred into nothing. The black sky and the black earth was a world tossed up-down as they walked towards something akin to freedom and the wind and rain that was mighty propelled them forward.

Trey wondered how long it would be before Wilder came with the guns. He wished for a little lost time to help them get ahead; push them through the fence and into a new world. It hadn't been long since Trey was in it, but it scared him all the same. He didn't belong in the lock-up, but he didn't belong in freedom fields either, not yet anyway.

'You're quiet,' he said to Kay.

'I'm thinkin.'

'Bout escapin?'

'Bout everythin, int hard to think bout everythin when you're out walkin blind in the dark, just bout anythin settles in the back of your mind.'

Trey and David agreed.

Every now and then Kay splashed the torchlight towards the fence for guidance and the rain became racing stars in the dark.

'We gotta find somethin soon,' she said. 'Can't keep walkin round in circles.'

'We int, I promise.'

She stopped and ran the light up and down the fence and the razor wire caught it dead in its scissor fingers.

'What is it?' asked Trey.

'Look.' She pointed the torch up towards the red light of one of the cameras. 'If the cameras are back on then the fence is on the same.' She picked up a rock and threw it at the wire and the three of them watched it buzz into momentary life.

Trey took a minute to rub the wet from his eyes and he rinsed his hat a hundred ways and slapped it back on his head.

'Listen,' he said and they all turned their ears in and out of the wind to catch the sound of something other than water hitting mud.

'That's gunfire,' said Kay.

The threat of adult violence made the war with Wilder a real war. No more kids with sticks battling over food rations but a fight for life.

Trey had friends and family in a mix-pot and something immediate in his life that wasn't back-pedalling revenge but some kind of forward fight. No loaded gun but a heart packed with purpose. If he survived this he could survive anything, he would survive everything. He wasn't a bad boy, bad things happened just because. Thought turned to his brother just then; living and growing and dying in a home that he could not call his own with people he would never call his own. This was war, a million times over it was war.

When the terror got too close he felt like shouting it gone and when it brought fear so uncontrolled he stopped with the shout surging through him and he wanted to scream so he might purge fully all the flame and fire that was in him. To purge was to cleanse, to live again.

When he thought the demon might return he tried to shake it from his flesh and marrow deep like a rabid dog. It was in that moment he realised the burn flaring up inside was nothing to be feared, it was love. Everything he was doing was for love.

'We got to get underground,' he said. 'And quick.'

They went on into the desperate night and there were times when the landscape took on other shapes and it moved in defiance despite the torrential rain and Trey told the others they were heading to where he had seen the underground trapdoor. Occasionally he recognised something of the landscape despite the floods and he thought to say and he kept his thinking to himself. If they could find the door that led from the quarry below ground then maybe they would have a chance of getting away.

They went tentatively on in a clutch about the quarry edge and steadied themselves ready for the unexpected. Their passage through the dead-night pits was slow and Trey's bare feet pounded with stupid side-step walking. Every now and then they stopped to let David snap strength back into his shoulders and they helped load the limp limpet boy once more on to his back.

Trey watched Kay check Lamby occasionally and he thought about those that were dead and he knew well that hook and twist of gut that turned you silent and void of self.

He also knew something of love, but pain resided there too and to him hurt was more powerful than love.

Occasionally gunfire sparked up the night sky and they stopped to watch the light tack splinters through the darkness; shooting stars fizzing and fading in the obscure night.

'You think he's killed anyone yet?' he asked Kay. 'Like shot someone killed someone.'

'Dunno,' she said. 'Probably just shootin off to show off.'

They both nodded and looked at the dangling boy hanging from David's back.

'Them shots are gettin closer,' he said and he looked at Kay and said he'd noticed it a while back. 'He'd have found the stables empty by now and knows we're still out here. Shootin's comin from that way.'

'Let's just keep goin,' said Kay suddenly. 'Let's just keep headin till there int no place left to head to.'

There were times when they thought perhaps they had been spared but then a single shot or shout would spring from nowhere and have them spun and coiled in fear.

When Trey finally found the trapdoor that led underground he shouted to the others to come over and through the rain he saw white eye glints flash hope through the dark.

They tried the door and it was locked from within and Kay jumped it to splitting and she kicked the wood until the hinges came clean away. Inside the cavity they were slow to descend the stairs and they entered the room below in a stumble and stood fixed in the thick dark and waited for Kay to switch on the torch.

'What you think this place is?' asked Trey.

'Storage room, I spose.'

'Storage for what, there int nothin here.'

'Everythin's been shipped out now, init? Nothin worth nothin left here.'

'You reckon it leads to the immigrants' quarters? The drugs factory?'

'Maybe,' said Kay. 'We just gotta hope it don't lead too

far back is all. At least it's someplace to hide out a while. We int got no choice in any case.' She looked at Trey and then at David. 'We agreed? We go in?'

The two boys nodded and the four of them headed deeper underground.

CHAPTER THIRTEEN

Beneath the underbelly of the moor the four youths took comfort in shelter from the storm.

To have the sound of rain no longer raging in their ears and the wet wiped from their eyes was to have a little of normality come back to them.

They descended further into the open gut wound and found another room cleared of whatever it was it had once stored and they sat circled to the tiny light for a few minutes' rest and they laid Lamby down against the wall.

What it was to be living was to know how close they were to dying all the same. 'We int done yet,' said Trey. 'While we're still breathin anyway.' He looked at Kay suddenly. 'We're lost, int we.'

'It's good to be lost,' she said. 'If we're lost it means we don't know if there's a way out and that's good. Means there might be.'

'Spose that makes sense, way you say it anyway.'

'Course. Everythin I say makes sense.' They both smiled and so did David and for a minute there was hope in happiness no matter how brief. They were alive, alive and going and thinking straight despite the cloistered creep of incarceration double deep.

They speculated about the reason for the tunnels and came up with nothing but illegality and Trey guessed those underground passages had been used for such a purpose for a long time, probably from the end of the mining boom when tin's worth fell and folks had to find other ways to survive. A hundred and more years down the line the country had turned back around to each and every man, woman and delinquent child for themselves.

'You reckon you could have had a better go at it if you'd bin given the chance?' He looked at Kay so she knew it was a proper question he was asking.

'Go at what?'

'Life,' he shrugged. 'Just life.'

'Spose. Too late now though. I was due a long run in this place and if we get out I'll be due a long run in another just like it.'

'Worse,' said David. 'Dead.' He got up and went to sit by Lamby because he was used to being part of a pair and the others had nothing more to add and they remained silent.

Trey thought about David's life up to that point and he thought about Kay and Lamby too and he knew this way of thinking about others was a good thing. Their lives had become his and his had partially stuck to theirs and the glue that was friendship was tar-tight.

He noticed Kay was watching the two boys and could see the worry in her and he wished that he could tell her he watched over her the same way if only from afar.

If she were not so thick-skinned he would have told her this, but she would have just laughed and told him to get lost. He knew the toughness that was in her head and heart and the way she went around pushing at the spaces that weren't hers.

Trey knew those scars on her shoulders had something to do with it and he thought to ask her about them and then he went ahead and flat-out said what was in his head.

'What bout em?'

'You got em all over?'

'My back, yes.' She looked at him and shrugged and said they weren't tribal markings if that was what he was wondering.

'Your mum did it,' said Trey. 'You don't have to say cus course she did.'

Kay shrugged. 'There you go then.'

'When?'

'When what?'

'When she do it?'

'Would be easier to say when she dint.'

'When she stop?'

'When she overdosed. She dint have so much use for that belt after that so I took it and when they put her in the ground I threw it in for a little memento of her life.'

'Spose heaven or hell she'll have a good bit of explainin to do.'

Kay shook her head. 'There was only one place that woman was headin and that was down.' She looked across at Trey and told him that he should rest a while.

'What bout you?'

'I int likely to sleep.'

'Me neither, not with Wilder and them stompin round above.'

They sat and watched the torchlight turn orange and then thin down to nothing and there was a moment when they kept to the dark and that dark was infinite. Trey closed his eyes to put the outside in and he took solace in just being; a thing and a nothing and an entity a part of everything. Lamby was right, they all had a shared hand in a science of sorts. He could hear the boy moan briefly through the pitch and he wondered what thought he might have in him that he might pass on to his friend to let him know everything was all right.

When Lamby moaned again Trey asked him what was wrong.

'Water,' said David.

'You lads OK?' asked Kay and she replaced the battery and flicked on the torch.

Trey took the torch from her and went to Lamby. 'The rain,' said Trey. 'It's comin through the wall.' He told David to carry Lamby away from the rising puddle and he bent to the crack in the mud wall with the rain water widening and threatening and he told the others it was probably time to head on. When he saw a rat and then another slip silent into the room he said there was no probability about it.

They advanced slow below the surface of the moor, a straggle-band of kids come together through circumstance a hundred times over and when they reached the next room they stopped.

'Looks like a dead end,' said Trey. 'There int nowhere else to go.'

'Wait.' Kay took back the torch and looped it across the concrete floor. 'There's somethin around that corner,' she said.

Trey watched Kay fade into the other side of the room and then he followed.

'Over here,' she shouted. 'Bloody knew it, it goes deeper underground.'

They both stood straddling the void where earth used to be.

'Don't go down there,' said Trey. 'You don't know what's down there.'

Kay tipped her toe at the edge and a little bit of grit scrambled free. They stood looking at the hole. It might be nothing, but it was definitely something.

'What you think's there?' asked Trey, one foot staged ready to step.

Kay shrugged. 'More of the same I 'spect, nothin and nothin again.'

'Could be a way out?'

Kay shrugged and she descended the steps in one jump. 'Hurry up the water's gettin higher.'

Trey followed Kay into the pool of light.

'It goes someplace,' she said.

'Where?'

'Someplace other than here and that'll do me.' She swung the torch and he could see the room was smaller than the ones upstairs. This was the entrance to the tunnels proper. They watched the light contract and crawl towards the passage and its strength was good but not so good that it would show the whole way.

Trey stood in the light beside her and something in him took pleasure in being her equal at last and he was about to speak when David shouted something about the gang above them.

'I'll go look,' said Trey. He climbed back up to the secret door despite the running rats for a quick look at the outside world.

The rain still slashed at the earth and lightning stabbed thin scissor-snap flashes towards the surrounding tors and the sporadic light made something of the black forever night.

247

A party was happening out there in the dark. Boys and girls who may once have been part friend or acquaintance danced rolling drunk and merry-mad through the muck and slop, wild things sniffing out a trail, good for the chase.

'They're half partyin, half huntin,' he said and he fixed the door behind him as best he could and he returned to the others and helped David heave Lamby on to his back and they followed Kay down the steps into the belly of earth.

They went slow, Kay upfront leading with the torch and Trey to the rear, occasionally flipping his lighter for the comfort cuddle, David bent to keep from knocking the boy against the low bump ceiling and the little light they had was lost at their feet.

'How close were them others?' asked Kay.

'Close.'

'How close?'

'Close and closin.'

'You think they know bout this place?'

'Dunno,' he said and he wished they could go a little faster in any case.

They went on and terror walked alongside them. Silence was a startling heartbeat in their ears and there were times when they thought they heard the sound of kids playing at soldiers trampling the ground above their heads.

Trey thought about the night his parents were killed and it was more than thought; he was back home hiding in the strange evening light, dust stars falling and circling all around, hope and heaven and hell settling, turning him, pumping his veins with bad-spirit blood, closing and trapping him within.

Trey kept walking, but in his mind he was fighting. Past, present and future at war with the scared little boy sitting inside and he told himself that today he would win; from now on he would always win. Each and every battle he would jump and stamp to his own drum and he would have his future return. The fight would no longer be a battle inside but in his hands where he could let it go. Despite everything he was getting somewhere with his thinking and he liked that.

'I got a plan,' he said and he stopped suddenly.

'What plan?' asked Kay and she shone the light on to his face.

'A plan I gotta do alone.' He looked at Lamby and told them they had to go on without him.

'Where you goin?' asked Kay.

'Back up.'

'Above ground? You int gonna do nothin stupid, are you?'

Trey nodded and said he hoped so.

'Don't be no hero.'

Trey shook his head and said that was one word that would never belong to him.

'I gotta do this,' he said. 'Prove I can do it.'

'You int got to prove nothin, not to me anyway.'

'To myself. I gotta do this, Kay, and you gotta let me.'

The two unlikely friends stood a moment and Trey wondered if she understood what he was asking and when she nodded that she did he smiled.

'Don't get killed,' she said and she turned her back and told David to follow her and he did.

Trey couldn't be sure if Wilder knew about the trap-door, but he couldn't risk him hunting down his friends. He took his time to retrace their footsteps and occasionally he flicked his lighter for small flame guidance. Up through the narrow gangways with the water shin-bone high he went on until finally he reached the steps that led to the door.

He held his breath a moment and listened out for the revellers through the hammer-hard rain and when he reckoned on the all-clear he pushed the broken door aside and crept out.

It felt odd to be back amongst the familiar, strange to have to spend one heartbeat more on the battleground, it was as if he was not done with dodging death.

He lay flat to the ground. His mouth a millimetre from mud and his eyes scanning the horizon, it was as if he himself was the sniper.

'Wilder,' he whispered. 'Wilder, where you at?' The sudden quiet was not what he expected. It unnerved him and he thought maybe the gang had found their tracks.

Trey pulled himself up on to his elbows and he took his time to crawl into the quarry. The further he was from the tunnels the better. He crawled and then he stooped and when he neared the quarry bottom with the puddle turned lagoon he stood and he ran until he reached halfway up the other side.

'Wilder,' he shouted. He listened. 'Wilder, where you at?'

He heard one lonely gunshot go up like a flare and he shouted his enemy's name until he saw the jagged shadow-line of heads frame the edge of the quarry.

Trey hoped his cousin would be stupid enough not to think to circle the pit. He thought for a moment that he would have to taunt him a little, throw some bait so he might come to him.

'Rudeboy,' Wilder shouted and he jumped from the side of the crater. Trey waited until his cousin was halfway down in the skid before he made the break.

He ran from the quarry where the gradient was less steep and on towards where he could see the outline of the camp buildings. Dawn was heading fast, pulling the rain clouds into hiding and replacing the dark with thin beginning light.

Trey could feel his heart beat crazy in his chest and his bare feet stung from the rock and stubble marshland and still he went on running.

Time was unimportant now. A few snatched minutes were all he had on Wilder and his gang, but with all their shouting and firing at Trey they were slow.

When he was near to the buildings he made sure to hide in the shadows. To go unnoticed was to keep from some gang wannabe telling all to Wilder. He went on.

Past the slaughterhouse and the bunkhouses and out across the clearing and when he saw the farmhouse he picked up speed and sprinted towards the back.

The things you notice in passing and the things you notice through obsession in the end only come down to one thing; memory when insight is needed. Trey had noticed the two-thousand-litre kerosene tank out the back of the house on his first day of camp walkabout; it had settled into the back of his mind and had made itself comfy, a dormant piece of information, until now.

The tank that was meant for warmth had a new destiny. It was meant for firing and a hundred times over it was meant for this.

Trey was quick to climb up to the tank and he turned the cap and the smell was catnip to him.

He could hear that the shouting was getting nearer, closing in on him with his fate perhaps at the whim of a trigger after all. He took his lighter from his pocket and rubbed his thumb across its calming steel one last time. It had become a part of him, had given him both guts and guidance, and here now it would be his sacrifice.

He flicked the flint for the last time, dropped it into the tank and ran for his life.

The explosion was enough to send Trey to the ground, enough to have his ears go deaf and his eyes blind a moment as he hit the wet earth.

He got up and despite everything he ran because he knew in that one brief minute the world had stopped turning so he might go on running. Wilder and Anders and all the kids in that camp on that moor would have stopped and stood and stared. This was his wormhole, his escape.

It was only when he reached higher ground that Trey dared stop and he allowed himself a moment's glory; fire not for the sake but for his future. He put his hand into his pocket with the lighter gone and he held on to the empty space and all the possibilities that in time might settle there. The lighter had done its job. The fire was going strong and Trey could see the flames dart up the side of the timber farmhouse, heading towards the rafters and hooking into every joist in its pursuit of destruction. He saw it glance occasionally from the windows, deciding which one then this one for the crack and slam. He thought about Wilder and knew all his hopes and dreams were in that melt of flame and fury, everything that boy had wished would soon be nothing more than an ashen memory of what could have been.

It was then that Trey turned towards the quarry and the tunnel. His eyes and heart and everything that was soul filled with the beauty of magnificent fire. It was all he would ever need, ever want.

He started to run when he realised dawn was upon him. He jumped the trapdoor and set the broken boards in place. Nothing would come between him and his freedom now, not even the pitch-black tunnel or the water that splashed hip high.

He waded on through the darkness, his feet pulsing with a hundred cuts and bruises and his hands outstretched for both balance and guard. With each step he felt the push and peel of the mud-clubbed walls and it was as if he were walking a tightrope strung between his past and his future. He hoped the tunnel had taken his friends somewhere safe and that it would guide him the same.

He went on and he dug his toes into the compact earth and he asked some god any god to guide him towards the place where his friends had passed by.

The fire that was in his heart filtered into his eyes and it lit up his future with a million possibilities. He glanced behind him to check for chasing signs but nothing followed.

The camp was behind them. Trey knew this because his new heart told him so. Hope had replaced all else and a cool wind blowing replaced the soul-fire, it was coming to him, closer and closer. Red had been replaced by blue, a hole at the end of the tunnel, getting closer and closing around.

Trey closed his eyes and felt the wind stretch out to greet him, its fingers about him, gathering, pulling him forward, leading him towards the light; a new day dawning, a new life waiting on the other side of the fence.

'You dead?' asked Kay. 'You breathin?'

Trey smiled and he opened his eyes and saw Kay and he smiled a hundred times over and he looked skyward to see a strip of paradise blue split and break the storm clouds into bubble pieces.

'Did we make it?' he asked and he went to sit up. 'Did we make it to the other side?'

'Take a look for yourself,' said Kay and she propped him up against a rock.

Trey looked down into the sharp cut of valley below and through the ridiculous fence towards the camp. From that distance he could see the compound in all its restrictive glory. He could see the flat-packed buildings and the ridge with the scrawny trees and the trenches dug ready for the secret haul things that would never be. Fires still smouldered and puffed out the wet night dregs and kids roamed in territorial packs, hunting for hunting's sake.

'How'd you get me up here?' he asked.

'David,' said Kay and Trey looked around to thank him but he was nowhere to be seen. He took some water and asked what had happened and he told her he remembered a lot of setting the fire and a little of running the dark tunnels, but nothing much more than that.

'You bashed your head comin out; David carried you up this hill, first Lamby and then you. Lucky to have a big lad like that on the team.'

'Where is everybody?'

'Gone.'

'Gone where?'

'You remember that track that brought you to camp?'

'Spose.'

'They headed that way, thought they might pick it up further down the line and then towards the main road.'

'Lamby still alive?'

'Just.'

'Spose he'd be dead by now if he was gonna die, he's lucky, guess we all are.'

Kay sat next to him and took out a box of matches from her pocket and opened it.

'What's that?' Trey asked.

'Cigarette.' She struck a match and lit it.

'Where you get that from?' he asked.

'Bin savin it.'

'For when?'

'For now.' She took a long drag and then passed it to Trey and he took it. 'Kept it for when we survived.'

'What if we hadn't?'

Kay looked at him and shrugged and Trey did the same. They both laughed.

'Spose I should thank you for savin me life.'

Trey nodded. 'Go on then.'

'What?'

'Thank me.'

Kay shook her head and she thanked him and took
the cigarette back into her hand.

'Spose you owe me one,' said Trey.

'You reckon?'

'I know it.'

'Don't get sappy on me now. Lamby was bad enough
with all the sad-sap.'

'That's true.' Trey smiled and he could have cried for
the sake of happiness. He let his heavy head fall into his
hands and shook out the sentimental mush. 'I feel like
crap,' he said.

'You look it.'

'My head hurts.'

'Course it does.'

They both laughed and Kay asked if he was ready to
get going.

'Not yet.'

'Take as long as you like.'

'I will.'

'Just don't take forever.'

'I won't.'

They sat in silence and watched the new dawn spiral
around them and colours settled like pools of dipping
rainbow water everywhere they looked. Trey thought
about their individual destinies laid out before them

beyond the moor, healing the bit of their hearts that hurt the most, and he thought about kin and he smiled. Maybe destiny was a thing after all.

'I got a brother,' he said suddenly. 'Spose you heard Wilder say somethin but, anyway, I got a brother.' He took a long drink of water and he settled back against the rock to tell Kay his story and about the Preacher and the words came rolling like spitting stones and he didn't know if they landed right or if they made any sense at all.

'You gettin any of this?' he asked.

Kay nodded. 'Why dint you tell me bout everythin earlier? Could have saved you a whole lot of heartache.'

'What you mean?'

'Revenge and all that, it's a big fat waste of time. Nothin ever comes of it; nothin ever comes from goin after a ghost.'

Trey passed the bottle of water and he took his time to get some way back on to his feet.

'Kay?' he asked. 'How you get to know so much bout everythin?'

'You jokin?'

'No really, seems there int nothin you don't know, seems you're right in all.'

Kay shrugged. 'You get to know a lot of things when you've had a life like mine, spose anyway. Thing is nothin but trouble comes from revenge. Trouble and heartache and a whole dump load of lost time.'

'Least I know I won't be goin after no one no more, Preacher or Wilder or some crazed junkie, none of it matters now.' He closed his eyes and as if for the first time memory came to him clear as parallel thinking. He saw the chapel cardboard black and cut out in a silhouette against the summer colour sky and the two coffins coming and passing and entering the gloom. Two coffins, Mum and Dad, and two people dead and all because of something maybe and nothing mostly.

'I never thought I was there,' he said suddenly.

'Where?' asked Kay.

'The funeral, had no memory or nothin, like it dint happen.'

He looked at her for one more answer and she told him it was denial and that was all.

'I dint want to believe it,' he said. 'Is that it?'

'You couldn't imagine it to believe it. Death's outside most kids' circle of thinkin.'

Trey thought about Mum and the way she sometimes came to see him in spirit and he knew it was all connected. He looked down towards camp and he looked beyond mere looking and saw the blue come clean and clear above their heads.

'Feels like somethin's been lost, somethin's been lost and found again.'

'Like the light,' said Kay and she started to pack the nothing bits that surrounded them into her sack bag.

'What you say?'

'Int that what Lamby says? It's science, somethin bout scattered light, the purer the sky the deeper the blue we're set for, the blue is the light that gets lost.'

'Why's the light lost?' asked Trey.

'The light at the blue end of the spectrum don't travel the whole way from the sun to us. It dissolves amongst the molecules in the air.'

Trey shrugged and there was something in her words that made sense. 'Spose a lot's been lost in all of us.' He nodded towards the wandering kids below them. Something of innocence had been separated from them all, separated and damaged and lost.

'We headin?' he asked.

'Spose, if you're up to it.'

'Course. Where to?'

'Same way as the others, towards whatever humanity can spare us.'

They descended the hill and were mindful of the compound and they circled it good and wide.

'So, you gonna walk in there and ask for that brother of yours or you plannin to spring him in the dark?' asked Kay.

'Dunno, int thought that far ahead in me thinkin.'

'You want some help? I'm good at pickin locks.'

'I wouldn't mind, if you int got no plans of your own.'

'Not much. Dint think I'd get out of camp anytime soon. It were somethin, weren't it?'

'Was somethin all right,' he agreed. 'Whole bloody camp thing was mental just about.'

Trey realised there was good and bad in the world, good and evil and all the roads that ran between. He had travelled them all, had walked them and backtracked them and he knew he'd never get a better chance at coming good than the road he was on. His friend beside him in the present and his brother waiting in the future and the demon that had him circled in fire was nothing to him now, nothing but bitter ashes in the past.

He looked towards the horizon and the blue sea waved him over; a good day was coming, a good life starting over.

By the same author

'Elegantly lyrical'
Independent
'A stone-cold stunner'
tor.com

Natasha
Carthew
winter
damage

BLOOMSBURY

'Elegantly lyrical'
Susan Elkin, *Independent*

OUT NOW